SEDONA'S
RED ROCK
RECIPES

by Eloise Carleton

Northland Publishing

www.northlandpub.com

Bound and printed in the United States of America

First Edition 1994

03   04   05   7   6   5   4

ISBN 0-87358-571-2

Cataloging-in-Publication Data
Carleton, Eloise, 1932-
Red rock recipes / by Eloise Carleton.—1st ed.
p.   cm.
Includes index.
1. Cookery, American—Southwestern style.
2. Cookery—Arizona—Sedona. I. Title.
TX715.2.S69C37 1994
641.5979—dc20   93-51503

Cover recipes: Mango Pineapple Salsa (page 106),
Flour Tortilla Baskets (page 37), and Simple Tostados (page 65).

The following Sedona restaurants contributed to this book:

Canyon Rose at Los Abrigados Resort
A Casalea
Enchantment Resort
The Heartline Café
La Mediterrannée
Oaxaca Restaurant and Cantina
Sedona Swiss
Willows Restaurant at Poco Diablo Resort Hotel

The following dear friends also contributed:

Debbie Banta
Jeannine Bethanis
Fran Bruno
Chris Carleton
Mitch Carleton
Sally Carroll
Bobbi Carlson
Beverly Castleberry
Elsie Close
Frank English
LeNoire Fish
Carolyn Flynn
Nancy Goerisch
Verlie Gregorson
Nancy Guth
Sharon Hogeland
Mary Jo Leader
Carol Hoffman Miller
Julie Moss
Marshall Moss
Henri Tubach
Joyce Vanderhoof
Dorothy Westwick
Sue Zanteson

To Betti Albrecht, who gave this novice a chance.
She has my heartfelt thanks. I hope she is pleased with the results.

Special thanks to my close friend and supporter,
Sharon Hogeland. You're a friend and a confidante!

And to my greatest inspiration, Sue Zanteson, thank you!

Contents

Introduction

S edona is a place of majestic beauty and tranquillity. People come to this red rock country from all walks of life to enter into a less complicated lifestyle and enjoy the creative environment here.

With the wonderful weather and great beauty of our area, there are many occasions for gathering friends together, and good food is often a part of these occasions.

This collection of recipes is for such gatherings of friends.

Some of these recipes are original to Sedona, and many have come here with people from other parts of the country and the world. Although this book is about southwestern cooking, that doesn't mean every meal consists of corn and chilies; tastes here are varied because of the influx of people from all over.

Most of these recipes are simple to prepare. Those that take longer can be done in easy steps ahead of time so gatherings of friends needn't be complicated by food preparation.

I hope you enjoy your visit to Sedona. And I hope these Red Rock Recipes will bring back memories of this special place long after you return home.

Bon appetít!

Cooking Notes

O ven temperatures given in this book are for a preheated oven (unless an individual recipe specifies starting in a cold oven).

When olive oil is specified, it should always be extra virgin. I recommend canola oil for regular cooking oil.

In most of these recipes, you can substitute margarine for butter; however, the flavor will be slightly different.

My personal preference is for less salt and more pepper, as you will see in many of these recipes. However, go by your own taste.

I recommend toasting nuts or seeds on a foil-covered rack in a toaster oven at 350°. If a toaster oven is unavailable, a pie plate in a regular oven will suffice. Monitor closely, about every 5 minutes, as every variety browns at a different pace.

I've used the following abbreviations: c. = cup, T. = tablespoon, t. = teaspoon, qt. = quart, pt. = pint, oz. = ounce, and pkg. = package.

Hors d'Oeuvres

Expinaca con Queso

from Oaxaca Restaurant and Cantina

2 oz. butter
1/2 c. chopped onion
1/2 bunch scallions, chopped
2 large cloves garlic, chopped
1 c. chopped cilantro
1 1/2 t. cumin
1 1/4 lb. fresh spinach
1 1/2 c. heavy cream
1 1/4 lb. jalapeño jack cheese, shredded

Melt butter in pan. Add onion, scallions, garlic, cilantro, and cumin; sauté until soft. Clean and chop spinach, and add to the onion mixture; stir until wilted. Add cream and simmer 25 minutes, stirring occasionally. Add cheese and stir well until melted. Serve hot with tortilla chips.

Artichoke and Olive Dip

1 14-oz. jar artichoke hearts,
drained and chopped
1 c. mayonnaise (regular or light)
1 c. (4 oz.) freshly grated parmesan cheese
1 clove garlic, minced
1 c. sliced ripe olives
2 T. chopped tomato

Combine the artichoke hearts, mayonnaise, parmesan cheese, garlic, and 3/4 c. olives. Spread in a 9" pie plate. Sprinkle with tomato and remaining olives. Preheat oven to 350° and bake uncovered for 20 minutes or until lightly browned. Serve with crackers or toasted pita chips. Serves 8.

For a southwestern flavor, replace the ripe olives with diced green chilies.

1 lb. ground beef (or ground turkey)
1/2 c. diced onion
2 c. salsa
32 oz. canned refried beans
1 1/2 c. grated cheddar cheese
3 avocados
1 T. lemon juice
1 c. sliced green onion
1/2 to 3/4 c. sour cream
1/2 c. sliced black olives
1/2 c. diced or sliced bell pepper (any color)
1/2 c. chopped fresh cilantro

Brown ground beef and onions in a skillet. Add salsa and simmer 5 minutes; then drain. Add salt and pepper to taste. Spread beans in bottom of a 9" x 13" baking dish. Cover with meat. Then sprinkle cheese over the meat. Mash avocados and combine with lemon juice and 1/2 c. of the green onions. Spread the avocado mixture over the cheese. "Stripe" the top with sour cream and arrange the remaining green onion and the black olives, bell pepper, and cilantro attractively over the top. Serves 16 to 20.

Sedona Fiesta Dip

Invite your guests to "scootch" through the dip with chips. Happy scootching!

1 c. sour cream

6 oz. cream cheese

2 T. butter, melted

1 T. cornstarch

1 T. grated onion

1/4 t. salt

1/4 c. dry vermouth

12 oz. fresh crab (or 2 cans, drained)

10 oz. cheddar cheese, grated

2–3 dashes hot sauce

paprika

chopped fresh parsley

Hot Crab Spread

*B*lend sour cream with cream cheese. Stir in melted butter, cornstarch, onion, salt, and vermouth. Gently fold in crab and cheddar cheese, reserving 1/4 c. cheddar cheese for topping. Spread mixture in ungreased 1-qt. baking dish. Top with remaining cheese and sprinkle with paprika. Bake 1 hour at 300°. Remove from oven and garnish with parsley. Serves 8 to 10.

2 lbs. brie cheese
1/2 c. jalapeño jelly
1/2 c. chopped green chilies
1/2 c. chopped fresh cilantro

Baked Southwestern Brie

R*emove rind from top of cheese and discard. Split cheese in half horizontally. Spread both halves with jalapeño jelly, then sprinkle chilies on top. Bake in preheated oven (350°) for 10 minutes. Remove and let stand for a short time. Top with cilantro and serve. Serves 12.*

This dish is a favorite. A bachelor friend who claims not to cook brings these to gatherings.

Francisco's Especiales

1 lb. mild mexican processed cheese spread
1 box of round 3" water crackers
1 c. chopped garnishes of your choice
(tomato, green chilies, black olives, fresh cilantro)

S*lice cheese and place on crackers. Garnish with any or all of the garnishes listed. Place on ungreased cookie sheet and bake at 350° for 8–10 minutes. Serves 12.*

12 hard-boiled eggs
1 t. white vinegar
1 t. honey
1/2 t. cumin
2 T. finely minced celery
2 T. minced green onion
1/2 c. diced green chilies
1 t. dijon mustard
salt and cayenne pepper to taste
mayonnaise to moisten
paprika
fresh cilantro leaves

*C*ut eggs in half horizontally (so ends of "cups" will stand up), *and remove egg yolks from whites. Combine egg yolks with vinegar, honey, cumin, celery, onion, chilies, mustard, paprika, salt,*

Huevos de Diablo

and cayenne pepper. Add enough mayonnaise to moisten and mix thoroughly. Scoop yolk mixture into egg-white cups. Sprinkle with paprika and garnish with cilantro leaves.

To make perfect hard-boiled eggs, place eggs in a pan and cover with water. Bring to a boil; cover and turn off heat. Set timer for 17 minutes. Remove eggs to bowl of ice water for 2 minutes, leaving cooking water in pan. Bring water in pan back to boil. Place eggs in boiling water for 10 seconds. Remove, crack shells, and peel under running water.

12 large (or 24 medium) mushrooms
lemon juice
2 T. butter
4 T. grated swiss cheese
1/4 lb. crab meat (or artificial crab)
1 T. minced fresh parsley
1 T. minced onion
4 T. dry sherry
dash of salt and black pepper
1/2 c. bread crumbs

W*ash mushrooms. Remove stems and set aside. Sprinkle each mushroom cap with lemon juice. Mince stems and sauté briefly in butter. Allow stems to cool, and add swiss cheese, crab meat, parsley, onion, sherry, salt, black pepper, and 1/4 c. of bread crumbs. Stuff mixture into mushrooms caps, and sprinkle with remaining 1/4 c. bread crumbs. Dot with a bit of butter, and bake at 350° for 25 minutes. Serves 12.*

Baked Mushrooms with Crab

1/3 c. lemon juice

1/3 c. oil

1/3 c. soy sauce

2 T. brown sugar

2 t. salt

2 t. black pepper

2 t. ground cloves

1 t. ground ginger

1 (4-lb.) pkg. chicken wing "drumettes"
(drumstick-shaped pieces of chicken wings)

sesame seeds

Combine first eight ingredients. Use to marinate chicken pieces for at least 3 hours. Spray a cookie sheet with nonstick cooking spray. Place chicken pieces on cookie sheet and sprinkle with sesame seeds. Bake in preheated oven at 350° for 40 minutes. Serves 12 to 16.

Wing Dings

1/2 c. flour
1 T. baking powder
12 eggs, well beaten
1 pt. cottage cheese
2 c. diced green chilies
1/2 lb. jack cheese, grated
1/2 lb. cheddar cheese, grated
1/4 lb. butter

*C*ombine flour and baking powder. Add eggs, cottage cheese, and green chilies. Combine jack and cheddar cheeses, reserving a third, and add the remainder to eggs.

Preheat oven to 400°. Put butter in a 9" x 13" baking dish and place in oven. After butter melts, pour egg mixture over butter, and top with reserved cheese. Place dish in oven, reducing heat to 350°. Bake 30–35 minutes. Dish is fully cooked when knife blade inserted in middle comes out clean.

If served as an entrée, cut into 4" squares and serve hot. If served as a hor d'oeuvre, chill and cut into 1" squares. Makes 6 main-dish servings or 12 hors d'oeuvres.

Chili Cheese Squares

ARTICHOKE VARIATION

Add 1 c. drained chopped marinated artichoke hearts.

$^1/2$ c. chicken broth
$^1/4$ c. butter
$^1/2$ c. bread flour
2 eggs
$^1/2$ c. diced chicken
$^1/4$ c. toasted almonds

H*eat chicken broth, and add butter. Bring to a boil, then add flour. Stir until mixture leaves the sides of pan and forms a ball. Remove from heat and use rotary beater to beat in eggs, one at a time. Add chicken and almonds to flour mixture. Drop by rounded teaspoonfuls on a greased cookie sheet. Bake in a preheated oven (400°) for 30 minutes. Makes 36 to 40.*

VARIATION #1

Substitute $^1/2$ c. crab or shrimp and $^1/4$ c. diced celery or water chestnuts for chicken and almonds.

Gougeré and Variations

VARIATION #2

Substitute $^3/4$ c. grated swiss cheese for chicken and almonds. Then sprinkle $^1/4$ c. grated swiss cheese over mounds on cookie sheet before baking.

Grated cheese ($^1/4$ c.) can be sprinkled over the first two recipes as well.

1/2 lb. fresh crab (or 2 cans, drained)
1 avocado, diced
2 T. sour cream
1/4 c. chopped green chilies
1 c. drained, peeled tomatoes, finely diced
salt and black pepper to taste
4 T. oil
8 flour tortillas
3/4 c. grated jack cheese

Combine crab, avocado, sour cream, chilies, tomatoes, salt, and black pepper. Heat oil in a heavy skillet on medium until hot. Fry tortillas one at a time, 10 seconds per side; remove from skillet. Spread 1/8 of crab mixture over each tortilla, and fold tortilla in half. Place tortillas on ungreased baking sheet, and sprinkle with cheese. Broil until the cheese melts. Remove and quarter tortillas. Serves 16.

Crab and
Avocado
Quesadillas

1/2 c. butter, melted
8 to 10 thin slices of fresh white bread
2 T. butter
2 T. flour
1 c. milk
2 eggs
1/4 c. grated swiss cheese
1/4 c. cream cheese, softened
1/4 c. grated parmesan cheese
parsley

B*rush inside surfaces of small muffin tin(s) with melted butter. Cut bread into 24 rounds, using a biscuit cutter. Place rounds in muffin tins, and brush bread with additional melted butter. Bake at 375° for 15 minutes.*

Melt 2 T. butter in small pan. Add flour and stir until mixture is smooth. Gradually add milk and cook until thick. Remove from heat. Beat eggs in a bowl, and quickly blend a few tablespoons of the hot milk mixture into the eggs. Then blend egg mixture into sauce in pan and cook for 1 minute. Add cheeses, mix thoroughly, and pile into toast cups. Bake at 350° for 7–10 minutes, or until golden brown and puffed. Garnish with parsley and serve. Makes 24 portions.

Filled Toast Cups

Great as an entrée with Cornville Corn Bread (page 34) and salad.

3 slices white bread
1/4 c. milk
2 lbs. ground beef
2 t. salt
1/4 t. black pepper
1 t. chili powder
1/2 t. dried oregano
2 eggs, lightly beaten
1/2 c. chopped onion
1 clove garlic, minced
2 T. olive oil
1 t. salt
1/4 t. dried oregano
1/4 t. cumin
10 oz. canned tomato purée

Southwestern
Meatballs

*S*oak bread in milk and mash with fork. Add beef, salt, black pepper, chili powder, oregano, and eggs, and mix well. Form into 1 1/2" balls and set aside.

Sauté onion and garlic in oil until golden brown. Add salt, oregano, cumin, and tomato purée. Simmer in a covered saucepan for 15 minutes, or until sauce thickens.

Add 1 c. water to sauce and bring to a boil. Add meatballs and reduce heat. Simmer meatballs in covered saucepan 35 minutes.

Serve with cocktail picks as an hors d'oeuvre or as an entrée over cornbread, noodles, or rice. Serves 12 to 16 as an hors d'oeuvre or 6 as an entrée.

This is not a difficult dish, but it is time consuming.
Your guests will be delighted and will beg you to make muffulettes again.

1 clove garlic, minced
1 T. dijon mustard
1 t. worcestershire sauce
2 T. red wine vinegar
1/2 T. dried basil (or 2 T. fresh)
1 t. crushed fennel seed
2 dashes hot pepper sauce
salt and black pepper to taste
1 c. olive oil
6 half chicken breasts
2 cloves garlic, minced
juice of 2 lemons
1 t. black pepper
6 anchovy fillets, rinsed

1/2 c. packed fresh
parsley leaves
1/4 t. dried basil
1/4 t. dried thyme
2 dashes hot pepper sauce
1 c. olive oil
2 c. spinach leaves, washed
2 red bell peppers
2 1-lb. baguettes
4 oz. canned sliced black olives
8 oz. feta cheese, crumbled
1 c. stemmed fresh basil leaves
4 (4" × 8") slices
provolone cheese

Muffulettes
(Stuffed Baguettes)

I n *food processor or blender, make marinade by combining garlic, mustard, worcestershire sauce, vinegar, basil, fennel seed, hot pepper sauce, salt, and black pepper. Then drizzle in oil until emulsified. Pound chicken breasts lightly to uniform shape and let stand in marinade overnight. Grill chicken on barbecue or under broiler until juices run clear. Let cool; then slice in half horizontally. Set aside.*

Make dressing in blender or food processor by combining garlic, lemon juice, black pepper, anchovy fillets, parsley, basil, thyme, and hot pepper sauce. Add olive oil gradually, and salt and pepper if desired. Continue blending until emulsified. Set aside.

Cut spinach leaves into chiffonade by rolling the leaves together and slicing them in 1/4" sections. Roast bell peppers by placing under the broiler until their skins are blistered on all sides; place in plastic bag for 15 minutes to steam. Peel and quarter peppers lengthwise.

Slice baguettes in half lengthwise and hollow out the middles, leaving shells 1/2" thick. Brush baguette halves with dressing. Layer two halves with spinach and drizzle with dressing. Overlap with slices of chicken. Cover with pepper slices, olives, feta cheese, basil leaves, and provolone slices.

Bake the filled baguette halves on an ungreased cookie sheet at 350° until provolone cheese starts to melt. Remove from oven and cover with reserved bread halves. Wrap tightly in plastic wrap, twisting ends, and refrigerate for at least 4 hours (up to 3 days).

Slice in 1" sections for hor d'oeuvres, or thicker for lunches or snacks.

Muffulettes
(Stuffed Baguettes)

Soups

46 oz. tomato-vegetable juice
I bell pepper, finely diced
I onion, minced
I cucumber, peeled, seeded, and finely diced
4 oz. diced green chilies
I T. worchestershire sauce
1/2 t. minced garlic
I T. olive oil
I T. chopped chives or scallions
dash hot pepper sauce

*C*ombine all ingredients. Salt to taste. Chill well. Garnish with lime wedges, avocado cubes, and garlic croutons. Makes 8 generous servings.

EASY SEAFOOD VARIATION

Marinate 1 c. scallops in 1 c. lime juice for 3 hours. Drain the scallops, then quarter and add to the above gazpacho recipe, along with 1/2–1 c. small cooked shrimp. Serve with bread.

Gazpacho

This dish goes very well with Chicken Almond Salad (page 49).

2 c. tomato purée
3 c. orange juice
2 t. sugar
zest of 1 orange, grated
zest of 1 lime, grated
1 mango or papaya, diced
2 c. diced cantaloupe
2 c. diced honeydew melon
1 apple, peeled and diced
1 c. blueberries
1 c. seedless grapes, halved
sliced strawberries and/or kiwi fruit

Combine the first six ingredients. Process half of mixture in blender or food processor until smooth. Combine with the remaining half and cantaloupe, honeydew, apple, blueberries, and grapes. Chill for several hours. Garnish with strawberries and/or kiwi fruit. Serves 8.

Fruit
Gazpacho

1 leek, sliced (discard green part)
2 large cucumbers, peeled, seeded, and sliced
2 T. butter
1 bay leaf
3 c. chicken broth
1 cucumber, peeled, seeded, and grated
1 c. cream
juice from 1/2 lemon
2 t. dried dill
salt and black pepper to taste
sour cream

Cold Cucumber Soup

*G*ently sauté sliced leek (white part) and sliced cucumber in butter with bay leaf for 20 minutes, or until tender but not browned. Add chicken broth and simmer 30 minutes. Remove bay leaf and purée in blender or food processor. Strain well, and add grated cucumber, cream, lemon juice, and dill. Chill. Season with salt and black pepper. Garnish with sour cream. Serves 8.

This soup is a favorite with guests.

1 lb. polish sausage, casings removed, sliced
1/2 c. chopped onion
1/4 c. chopped bell pepper
1/3 c. butter
2 T. flour
1 1/2 t. black pepper
1 T. dried parsley flakes
1/2 bay leaf
1/4 t. poultry seasoning
3 c. milk
32 oz. canned cream-style corn
16 oz. canned sliced potatoes

Simmer sausage in boiling water 5 minutes, drain, and set aside. Sauté onion and bell pepper in butter. Blend in flour and seasonings and cook until bubbly. Add milk gradually and stir until smooth. Add corn and potatoes, and continue cooking until thick and creamy. Add sausage. Remove bay leaf. Serves 6.

Corn Chowder

1 onion, chopped
2 cloves garlic, minced
1 T. oil
1/4 t. freshly ground black pepper
1/2 t. cumin
1/2 t. oregano
2 potatoes, peeled and cubed
2/3 c. diced green chilies
4 c. chicken broth
chopped fresh cilantro
shredded jack cheese

Sauté onion and garlic in oil until soft. Stir in black pepper and cumin; cook 2 minutes. Add oregano, potatoes, chilies, and chicken broth. Simmer 45 minutes, or until potatoes are tender. Garnish with cilantro and jack cheese. Serves 4.

Chili Potato Soup

2 1/2 lbs. winter squash, peeled
1 c. chopped onion
2 T. butter
1 T. fresh sage (or 1 t. dried)
pinch of allspice
1 cooking apple, peeled, diced
2 T. lemon juice
1 qt. chicken stock
1/4 c. toasted walnuts

Bake squash until tender. Meanwhile, sauté onion in butter. Add sage, allspice, apple, lemon juice, and chicken stock. Simmer 25 minutes or until apple is tender. Purée squash in blender or food processor. Add to soup and simmer a few minutes before serving. Garnish with walnuts. Serves 6.

Squash Soup

1 large onion, diced
2 carrots, peeled and diced
4 stalks celery, finely diced
4 slices bacon, chopped, fried until soft
4 T. flour
32 oz. canned clams (whole or chopped)
1 (8-oz.) bottle clam juice
4 c. peeled and cubed potatoes
1 bay leaf
3 c. milk
2 c. half-and-half
2 T. butter
dash hot pepper sauce
salt and black pepper to taste
8 oz. green chilies (optional)

Sedona-Style Clam Chowder

Sauté onion, carrots, and celery with fried bacon until soft. Add flour and juice from clams. Add bottled clam juice and cook until slightly thickened. Add potatoes and enough water to submerge them. Add bay leaf and cover pot; cook over low heat until potatoes are tender (30–45 minutes). In a separate pot, scald milk and half-and-half, then add butter and clams. Add hot milk mixture and hot pepper sauce to chowder and season to taste. Add chilies if desired. Simmer gently for 10 minutes. Remove bay leaf. Serve immediately. Serves 8 to 10.

1/2 lb. ground beef
1/2 c. chopped onion
16 oz. canned pinto or chili beans
16 oz. stewed tomatoes
8 oz. tomato sauce
1 1/2 c. water
1/2 pkg. dry taco seasoning mix
4 oz. diced green chilies
garnishes

Brown meat and onion. Add beans, tomatoes, tomato sauce, water, taco seasoning, and chilies. Simmer 20 minutes. Garnish with any or all of the following; sliced avocado, shredded cheddar cheese, sliced green onion, sliced black olives, corn chips, and sour cream. Serves 4.

Taco Soup

1 large onion, chopped
4 cloves garlic, minced
4 T. oil
1 lb. dried black beans, rinsed
6 c. chicken broth
28 oz. crushed tomatoes
1 jalapeño chili, finely chopped
2 T. ground red chilies (or chili powder)
2 T. chopped fresh cilantro
1 T. crumbled dried oregano
2 t. ground cumin
sour cream
additional fresh cilantro
chopped yellow or red bell pepper

Southwestern Spicy Black Bean Soup

Cook onion and garlic in oil until tender. Add beans, broth, tomatoes, jalapeño, and spices. Bring to boil; reduce heat and simmer for 2 1/2–3 hours, or until beans are tender. Allow to cool. Blend mixture with blender or food processor until smooth. Reheat and garnish with sour cream, cilantro, and bell pepper. Serves 8.

2 c. water
14 1/2 oz. beef broth
14 1/2 oz. chicken broth
14 1/2 oz. tomatoes, chopped
1/2 c. chopped onion
1/4 c. chopped green pepper
2 large whole chicken breasts, boneless, skinned
8 3/4 oz. whole kernel corn, drained
1 t. chili powder
1/2 t. ground cumin
1/8 t. ground black pepper
3 c. coarsely crushed tortilla chips
4 oz. monterey jack cheese, shredded
1 avocado, peeled, seeded, and cubed
snipped fresh cilantro (optional)
lime wedges (optional)

Tex-Mex Tortilla Soup

In a large saucepan, combine water, beef and chicken broth, undrained tomatoes, onion, and green pepper. Bring to a boil. Cut chicken into 1" cubes and add to saucepan. Reduce heat, cover, and simmer for 10 minutes. Add corn, chili powder, cumin, and black pepper. Simmer, covered, for 10 more minutes. Place crushed tortilla chips into bowl and ladle soup over chips. Sprinkle with cheese, avocado, and cilantro. Serve with lime wedges. Serves 6.

Muy bien!

2 c. dried hominy (or 3 cans, drained)
1 large onion, chopped
1 clove garlic, minced
2 T. oil
juice of 1 lime
8 oz. diced green chilies
2 jalapeño peppers, diced
2 qts. water
1 lb. shredded cooked pork (page 76)
1/4 t. dried oregano
2–3 t. salt
black pepper to taste

Posolé

If using dried hominy, soak in water overnight, then drain before starting. In a dutch oven, sauté onion and garlic in oil. Add hominy, lime juice, chilies, and jalapeños. Submerge in water (or broth from pork), and simmer until hominy opens. Add pork and seasonings. Simmer 30 minutes.

If using canned hominy, add to dutch oven with onion mixture, lime juice, chilies, and jalapeños, and simmer 30 minutes. Add water or broth if necessary. Add pork and seasonings, and simmer until flavors are well blended. Serves 8.

This dish is my own creation. I hope your family enjoys it as much as mine does.

1 lb. italian sausage (mild or spicy)
1 large onion, chopped
2 cloves garlic, minced
16 oz. prepared pasta sauce
16 oz. crushed tomatoes
13 oz. chicken broth
1 T. dried basil
salt and black pepper
12–16 oz. tortellini, cooked slightly less time than directed
freshly grated parmesan cheese

B*rown sausage, onion and garlic in dutch oven. Add pasta sauce, tomatoes, chicken broth, and basil. Simmer for 45 minutes. Season to taste. Add cooked tortellini, and simmer 10 more minutes. Garnish with parmesan cheese and serve with hot garlic bread. Serves 6.*

Tortellini
Soup

Breads

from Sedona Swiss Restaurant and Café

1 1/4 c. lukewarm water
1/3 oz. bakers yeast
5/8 c. medium rye flour
1/2 c. bread flour
3 c. cold water
1 1/2 oz. bakers yeast
5 c. bread flour
1 1/4 c. medium rye flour
2 T. salt

Mix first four ingredients. Cover and let sit overnight. Add next four ingredients and mix well. Add salt and mix thoroughly. Cover with cloth and let rise. When tripled in size, cut into 6 parts. On a board or table dusted with flour, knead a few times and shape into loaves. Cover with damp cloth and let rise 30–45 minutes. Place on baking sheet. Bake at 300° about 1 hour.

House Bread

These are heavenly with soup and/or salad.

1 c. flour
1/2 t. mexican seasoning (or chili powder)
1/4 t. garlic salt
1 T. melted butter
1 c. milk
3 eggs
1 c. grated cheddar cheese
1/4 c. chopped ripe olives

Combine flour and seasonings in bowl. Add butter, milk, and eggs and beat at medium speed for 2 1/2 minutes. Add cheese and olives, and continue beating. Fill large, greased muffin cups (1/3–1/2 c. size) no more than two-thirds full. Bake on center rack of oven at 375° for 45–50 minutes, or until well browned and firm to the touch. If a drier texture is desired, loosen popovers and set ajar in muffin tin, leaving them in the warm oven with the heat off and the door partially open for an additional 8–10 minutes. Makes 12 popovers.

Cheddar Cheese Popovers

You can also add 1/4 c. diced green chilies or replace the olives with green chilies.

1 c. yellow cornmeal
1 c. canned cream-style corn
3/4 c. milk
1/2 t. salt
1/2 t. baking soda
1/3 c. oil
2 eggs, beaten
2 c. grated cheddar cheese
4 oz. diced green chilies

*C*ombine cornmeal, corn, milk, salt, baking soda, oil, and eggs. Pour half the batter in a greased 9" x 9" pan, then sprinkle on half of the cheese. Lace the top with chilies and cover with remaining cheese. Pour remaining batter on top, and bake at 400° for 35 minutes. Cut into squares. Can be served hot or at room temperature. Serves 12.

Cornville Corn Bread

CORN HUSK MUFFIN VARIATION

Place 24 dried corn husks in very hot water and soak for a few hours. Drain and remove all silk; cut husks into 1" x 4" pieces. Prepare corn bread batter. Grease 12 muffin cups or spray with non-stick cooking spray. Crisscross 4 corn husk pieces in each cup. Pour half of the batter in equal amounts into the muffin cups. Sprinkle on half of the cheese and layer with chilies. Pour the remaining batter on top. Top with remaining cheese. Cap with a small pitted ripe olive, if desired. Bake at 350° for 15–20 minutes. Serves 12.

These are a fine accent for soups.

2 T. butter
3/4 lb. cheddar cheese, grated
1 t. worcestershire sauce
3 T. grated onion
dash cayenne pepper, to taste
2 eggs
4 oz. diced green chilies
1 loaf french bread, cubed (about 60 cubes)

M*elt butter and cheese in a double boiler. Add worcestershire sauce, onion, and cayenne pepper, and let cool. Beat eggs in separate bowl; fold in chilies. Mix eggs into cheese mixture.*

Dip bread cubes in cheese mixture, shaking off excess. Place on wax paper to drain. Then place on an ungreased cookie sheet and bake at 350° for 10–12 minutes.

If cheese cubes are to be served later, place the dipped cubes in a bag and freeze. When using frozen cubes, allow additional baking time.

Chili Cheese Cubes

Pita Toast

1 T. fresh snipped dill (or 1 t. dried)
1 T. minced fresh parsley
1 large clove garlic, minced
juice of 1/2 lemon
1 1/2 sticks butter, melted
6 large pita rounds

Combine dill, parsley, garlic, lemon juice, and melted butter. Separate pita rounds horizontally and brush butter mixture on the inside of each half. Cut each into six pieces, then place each piece on an ungreased baking sheet with the buttered side up. Bake at 450° for 5 minutes, or until lightly browned and crisp. Makes 72 pieces.

Corn Pancakes

1 1/4 c. cornmeal
1/4 c. flour
1/2 t. salt
1/2 t. black pepper
1/2 t. baking powder
2 c. buttermilk
2 eggs, lightly beaten
3 T. oil
1 1/2 c. corn kernels (fresh, frozen, or canned)

In a large bowl, combine cornmeal, flour, salt, pepper, and baking powder. In a second bowl, mix buttermilk, eggs, and oil. Add to dry ingredients, and gently stir in corn. Mix thoroughly. Place 2 T. of batter on a hot nonstick skillet. Fry 2 minutes on each side. Serve with beans. Serves 4.

10" flour tortillas
oil

Brush both sides of each tortilla with oil. Preheat oven to 375°. Drape tortillas over ovenproof bowls and place on cookie sheets. Bake until lightly brown, about 10 minutes.

If fluted molds are available, press tortillas into molds and bake as above.

Use these for taco and other salads.

DESSERT TORTILLA BASKETS

Trim small (fajita-sized) flour tortillas with ravioli cutter, and brush both sides with oil. Press into large muffin cups or small fluted molds. Sprinkle with sugar and/or cinnamon (1 T. cinnamon to 1/4 c. sugar). Bake as above.

Flour Tortilla Baskets

Salads and Dressings

1 head romaine lettuce
1 head curly or red leaf lettuce
1 red bell pepper, julienned
1 c. sliced green onion
4 pepperoncini peppers, seeded and sliced thinly
8 oz. pitted black olives
6 plum tomatoes, peeled and sliced thinly
1 small red onion, sliced thinly and ringed
6 oz. provolone cheese, julienned
6 oz. salami, julienned
1 c. Italian Dressing (page 50)
1 c. freshly grated parmesan cheese

Remove tough ends of lettuce leaves. Wash leaves and spin dry; tear into bite-sized pieces. Toss all ingredients, adding parmesan cheese last. Grind black pepper over salad. Serves 12.

Antipasto Green Salad

2 t. dried dill weed
1/2 c. yogurt
1/2 c. sour cream
1 large clove garlic, minced
1/2 t. salt
1/2 t. freshly ground black pepper
1 lb. frozen baby peas, thawed and drained
1/2 c. sliced radishes
1/4 c. chopped green onion
1 stalk celery, diced
1/2 c. spanish peanuts
6 slices bacon, cooked and crumbled

*W*hisk *dill weed, yogurt, sour cream, garlic, salt, and black pepper in bowl. Add peas, radishes, onion, and celery. Chill 4 hours. Garnish with peanuts and bacon. Serves 6.*

Pea Salad

This salad keeps for days and is great for picnics.

3/4 c. white vinegar
3/4 c. sugar
1/2 c. oil
1 t. celery seed
32 oz. canned french-style green beans
12 oz. canned white corn niblets
17 oz. can baby peas (or 2 c. frozen baby peas)
1 c. chopped celery
1 (4-oz.) jar diced pimento
1/4 c. minced green onion
1 c. diced red, green, or yellow pepper

Marinated Vegetable Salad

For dressing, combine vinegar, sugar, oil, and celery seed, and cook over medium heat until sugar is dissolved. Cool. Drain canned vegetables and add to fresh. Combine with dressing and marinate. Serves 12 to 14.

House guests love this salad.

1–2 c. vegetables (frozen baby peas, asparagus,
green beans, and/or broccoli florets)
1 lb. linguini, broken in thirds, cooked and cooled
4 green onions, chopped
1/2 c. minced parsley
2 tomatoes, peeled, seeded, and chopped
1/2 c. sliced ripe olives
1/2 c. chopped bell pepper
1 T. dry italian herb seasoning
8 oz. Italian Salad Dressing (page 50)
salt and black pepper to taste

B*lanch vegetables (except frozen peas) in boiling water,
then drain. (Vegetables should still be crisp.) Combine all
ingredients and chill at least 4 hours. Serves 12.
Peas can be used right out of the freezer with
no cooking.*

Pasta Salad

Broccoli Salad

Try this unusual salad; it may become a favorite.

1/4 c. sugar
2 T. cider vinegar
1 c. mayonnaise
4 c. broccoli florets,
blanched in boiling water 2 minutes
4 green onions, chopped
6 slices bacon, cooked crisp and crumbled
1/2 c. golden raisins

Combine sugar with vinegar and heat in microwave until dissolved. Allow mixture to cool. Add mayonnaise. Combine with the remaining ingredients and chill salad for 2–3 hours. Serves 6.

Southwestern Coleslaw

This salad is perfect with Mexican entrées.

2 cloves garlic, minced
1/2 c. vinegar
1/4 c. oil
2 T. sugar
salt and black pepper to taste
1 head cabbage, shredded
1 green pepper, diced
6 stalks celery, diced
10 oz. canned corn with peppers
3 tomatoes, peeled, seeded, and diced

One day before serving, whisk together garlic, vinegar, oil, sugar, salt, and black pepper. Combine with vegetables. Cover and refrigerate (for up to two days). Serves 6.

from Heartline Café

1/2 c. vegetable oil
2/3 c. hazelnuts
2 medium heads red cabbage,
cored and sliced thin
1/2 t. salt
1/3 c. balsamic vinegar
2 pears or apples, cored and sliced
1 small log fresh goat cheese

Warm Red Cabbage Salad with Hazelnuts and Goat Cheese

*I*n a medium-sized roasting pan, heat oil on
the stove or in oven. When the oil is hot, add
hazelnuts and cabbage. Stir until wilted, then add salt and vinegar.
Place sliced apples or pears around the edges of serving plates.
Scoop the warm cabbage into the middle of each plate and put a
piece of goat cheese on top. Serves 6.

2 lbs. small red potatoes
1 large red onion, chopped
4 T. fresh dill weed, minced (or 2 T. dried)
1/2 c. Italian Salad Dressing (page 50)
1/2 c. mayonnaise
1/2 t. dijon mustard
1 T. balsamic vinegar
salt and black pepper to taste

Red Potato Salad

*S*crub potatoes, and slice or quarter them. Cook until tender
when pierced with a fork. Combine with onion and dill.
Combine italian dressing, mayonnaise, mustard, vinegar, salt, and
black pepper, and pour over potatoes. Add additional dressing if
salad is dry. Chill. Serves 10.

Beet Horseradish Salad

Great with beef dishes.

16 oz. canned julienned beets
1 (3-oz.) pkg. lemon gelatin
(low calorie is acceptable)
3 T. vinegar
1/2 t. salt
2 T. grated onion
3/4 c. minced celery
2 T. prepared horseradish
lettuce leaves

Drain liquid from beets and add water to make 1 1/2 cups. Add gelatin. Heat with the vinegar to dissolve gelatin. Add salt and onion. Chill until mixture is partially set. Add celery and horseradish, and chill in a 8" pan. Cut in squares and serve on beds of lettuce leaves. Serves 6.

Grapefruit and Blue Cheese Salad

4 grapefruit, peeled and sectioned
spinach leaves, washed and stemmed
1/4 c. sliced green onion
4 oz. blue cheese, crumbled
1/2 c. Sherry or Raspberry Walnut Dressing
(page 50)

Arrange grapefruit sections on a bed of spinach leaves. Sprinkle on green onions and blue cheese. Drizzle with dressing. Serves 4.

To section grapefruit or oranges, peel with a sharp knife so no white pith is left. Holding fruit in your hand over a bowl to catch juices, slice next to the membranes, down and up, to remove sections.

1 1/2 lb. small beets (homegrown, if possible)
1/2 c. vinegar
4 green onions, chopped
1/2 c. diced celery
1/2 c. diced green bell pepper
1/2 c. chopped walnuts
2 cloves garlic, minced
1/3 c. walnut oil
3 T. raspberry vinegar
salt and black pepper to taste

Summer Beet Salad

*S*crub beets and remove tops and ends. Put in saucepan with vinegar, and add enough water to cover. Cook until tender, and drain. When beets have cooled enough to handle, remove skins under running water. Cut in 1/2" cubes. Combine beets with the remaining ingredients and allow to marinate at room temperature for 2 hours. Serve on a bed of bibb lettuce leaves.

2 cucumbers
1/4 c. seasoned rice vinegar
1/4 t. salt
1/4 lb. cooked shrimp, sliced horizontally

Cucumber Salad

*P*eel cucumber and slice thin. Add vinegar, salt, and shrimp. Marinate at least one hour. Spoon egg sauce over each serving if desired. Serves 4.

EGG SAUCE

Mash 3 hard-cooked egg yolks with 1 T. sugar, 1/8 t. salt and 1 T. seasoned rice vinegar. Gradually mix in an additional 1 1/2 T. vinegar until mixture has a smooth paste-like texture.

Orange and Onion Salad

20 button mushrooms, washed and stemmed
1 c. Mint Dressing (page 50)
2 heads red leaf lettuce, washed and dried
2 red onions, peeled and sliced thinly
6 oranges, peeled and sliced thinly

Marinate mushrooms in dressing for 4 hours. Place lettuce leaves on platter or individual serving plates. Arrange onion rings, orange slices, and mushrooms on top. Pour on remaining dressing. Garnish with mint sprigs. Serves 10.

Spinach Strawberry Salad

1 package pre-washed spinach, stemmed and torn into bite-size pieces
1 pt. fresh strawberries, washed, hulled, sliced, and dried on paper towels
1/2 c. thinly sliced green onion
1/2 c. Sherry or Raspberry Walnut Dressing (page 50)

Combine spinach, strawberries and green onion. Pour dressing over salad, and grind fresh black pepper on top. Toss. Serves 6.

1 pkg. non-instant wild and brown rice mix
1/2 c. mayonnaise
2 T. curry powder (or more, to taste)
8 oz. marinated artichoke hearts
(reserve liquid)
4 oz. black olives, sliced
4 green onions, sliced

Wild Rice
Artichoke
Salad

Cook rice as directed on package without butter. Mix mayonnaise with artichoke marinade and add curry to taste. Chop artichoke hearts, and combine with rice, mayonnaise, olives and onions. (If mixture seems dry, add a bit more mayonnaise.) Chill. Serves 6.

A large flowering kale leaf makes a nice container for this salad.

This salad may be used as an easy entrée.
It may also be frozen and then defrosted for later use.

Chicken
Almond
Salad

1 T. gelatin
1/4 c. cold water
1 c. mayonnaise
1 c. heavy cream, whipped
1/2 t. salt
2 c. diced cooked chicken
3/4 c. sliced pimento-stuffed green olives
3/4 c. toasted slivered or sliced almonds

Soften gelatin in cold water. Then place gelatin mixture in double boiler over hot water and heat until gelatin is dissolved. Cool and add to mayonnaise, whipped cream, and salt. Fold in remaining ingredients. Chill in mold until firm. Serves 6.

Italian Dressing

1/4 c. olive oil
2 T. red wine vinegar
1 t. dry mustard
1/2 t. salt
1/2 t. black pepper
1/4 c. grated parmesan cheese

Whisk all together or combine in blender.

Mint Dressing

2 c. finely chopped mint
1/2 c. red wine vinegar
1/2 t. salt
1/2 t. black pepper
1 1/2 c. olive oil

Combine mint, vinegar, salt, and pepper in blender. Add oil in a stream. Refrigerate.

Raspberry Walnut Dressing

1 clove garlic, minced
1/4 c. raspberry vinegar
1 T. dijon mustard (optional)
1/4 t. salt
3 T. walnut oil
1/2 c. canola oil

Whisk garlic, vinegar, mustard, and salt together. Add oils in a stream; continue whisking until emulsified.

1 egg
1/4 t. salt
2 c. olive oil
2 c. canola oil
1/2 c. vinegar
1/2 c. cream sherry
1 clove garlic, minced

Sherry
Dressing

Whisk egg and salt together. Add oils and vinegar alternately, whisking well. Slowly whisk in sherry and garlic. Makes 5 cups. For fruit salads, omit garlic and add 1 T. sugar.

2 cloves garlic, minced
juice of 2 lemons
1 t. black pepper
6 anchovy filets, rinsed
1/2 c. packed parsley leaves
1 t. dijon mustard
2 dashes hot pepper sauce
1/4 t. dried basil
1/4 t. dried thyme
1 c. olive oil

Anchovy
Parsley
Dressing

Process all ingredients in blender or food processor, adding oil in a steady stream.

This dressing is excellent brushed over french or sourdough bread and baked at 350° for 10 minutes.

Fish and Seafood

1/4 c. cornmeal
1/4 c. flour
pinch of salt and black pepper
4 5-oz. fish filets, 3/4" thick
2 T. oil
1/3 c. sour cream
2 T. chopped green chilies
1/3 c. shredded jack cheese
chopped parsley
paprika

Combine cornmeal, flour, salt, and black pepper. Dredge fish through cornmeal mixture. Place fish in a oiled skillet, and fry over medium high until golden brown on each side (about 5 minutes per side), or until fish flakes easily. Combine sour cream, chilies, and cheese. Pour over fish and place 6" beneath a preheated broiler. Broil 3 minutes, or until lightly browned. Sprinkle with parsley and paprika. Serves 4.

Mexicali Fish

15 $^1/_2$ oz. salmon, drained
2 c. soft bread crumbs
2 eggs, lightly beaten
$^1/_2$ c. grated cheddar cheese
$^1/_4$ c. salsa verde
$^1/_4$ c. minced green onions
dash hot pepper sauce
salt
ground black pepper
1 T. butter or margarine, melted

Combine salmon, crumbs, eggs, cheese, salsa, onions, hot pepper sauce, salt, and black pepper. Form into 6 patties. Brush each with butter, and broil 3" from preheated broiler until brown on both sides (approximately 3–4 minutes per side). Serves 4 to 6.

Broiled
Salmon
Patties

1 zucchini, sliced
1 small eggplant, peeled and diced
2 T. olive oil
2 cloves garlic, minced
1 t. freshly crumbled thyme leaves (or $^1/_2$ t. dried)
1 t. ground cumin
4 roma tomatoes, peeled, seeded, and chopped
$^1/_3$ t. salt
$^1/_2$ t. black pepper
4 5-oz. fresh tuna or ahi steaks
1 t. lemon juice
1 T. fresh basil, minced (or $^1/_2$ t. dried)

Grilled Tuna with Nicoise Sauce

In a heavy skillet, sauté zucchini and egg-plant in half of the olive oil. Add garlic, thyme, cumin, tomatoes, and half salt and black pepper. Bring mixture to a boil. Then bake at 375° for 25 minutes. Cool. Slice tuna into $^1/_2$" slices and marinate in nicoise sauce (the lemon juice, basil, and remaining salt, black pepper, and olive oil) for 10 minutes. Grill on barbecue approximately 2 to 3 minutes per side. Pour zucchini and eggplant mixture on top. Serves 4.

Parslied red potatoes and a simple salad are nice finishing touches.

2 T. minced garlic

3 T. olive oil

2 T. flour

15 oz. canned clams, drained (reserve juice)

1 T. lemon juice

$1/2$ c. dry vermouth

salt and black pepper to taste

1 lb. linguine, cooked

$1/2$ c. chopped fresh parsley

1 c. freshly grated parmesan cheese

*S*auté garlic in oil. Add flour and brown. Whisk in clam juice, lemon juice, and vermouth. Continue whisking over medium heat until mixture thickens. Add additional vermouth if necessary. Add clams, salt, and black pepper. Pour over hot linguine and garnish with parsley and cheese. Serves 4.

Quick Clam Sauce for Linguine

3/4 lb. mushrooms, sliced
1 T. chopped onion
2 T. butter
2 cans cream of mushroom soup
1 pt. sour cream
1/4 c. vermouth
2 t. worcestershire sauce
1 t. curry powder
1 t. chopped parsley
pinch dried oregano
pinch paprika
dash salt and black pepper
2 lb. shrimp, cooked
12 oz. spinach noodles,
cooked and drained
1/2 c. grated cheddar cheese

Shrimp and Green Noodle Casserole

In a large saucepan, brown mushrooms and onion in butter. Add soup, sour cream, vermouth, worcestershire sauce, curry powder, parsley, oregano, paprika, salt, and black pepper. Then add shrimp and noodles and pour into a greased 3-quart casserole or 9" x 13" baking dish. Top with cheese and bake at 350° for 35 minutes. Serves 6 to 8.

This dish must be prepared the day before.

3 c. sliced leeks
3 T. butter
5 eggs
2 $1/2$ c. milk
salt and black pepper
7 slices sourdough bread
I lb. cooked bay shrimp (or larger shrimp,
sliced in half lengthwise)
I lb. swiss cheese, grated
3 T. snipped fresh dill weed (or I $1/2$ T. dried)

S *auté leeks in butter. Whisk eggs with milk, salt, and black pepper. Remove crusts from bread; butter the slices, and cut into cubes. Place bread cubes in a 9" x 13" greased baking dish. Top with leeks, shrimp, cheese, and dill weed. Pour egg mixture on top, and refrigerate overnight. Bake at 350° for 1 hour. Allow to stand for 10 minutes and serve.*

Shrimp
Strata

This recipe requires many steps; however, the reward is worth the effort.

2 T. butter
2 T. flour
1/2 t. dijon mustard
3/4 c. milk
2 T. heavy cream
salt and black pepper to taste
1 c. fine dry bread crumbs
1/4 c. parmesan cheese
1/4 t. dry mustard
1/2 lb. phyllo pastry sheets
(if frozen, defrost in
refrigerator overnight)
3/4 c. melted butter

1 lb. crab, shrimp
or other seafood, cooked and
cut in bite-sized pieces
1/2 c. grated swiss cheese
2 hard-boiled eggs, chopped
3/4 c. sour cream
1/4 c. chopped parsley
1/4 c. chopped shallots
2 T. chopped chives
1 clove garlic, minced
2 T. freshly grated
parmesan cheese
1 t. chopped parsley

Seafood Strudel

Melt butter and blend in flour. Cook 2 minutes and remove from heat. While stirring, add mustard and milk. Return to heat and stir until mixture comes to a boil. Boil 1 minute. Add cream and season to taste. Cover and chill for 2 hours.

Combine bread crumbs, parmesan cheese, and dry mustard in a bowl. Set aside.

Carefully unroll phyllo sheets. (Note: Keep sheets moist by covering with waxed paper and a damp towel. Remove sheets one at a time.) Brush with melted butter and sprinkle with bread crumb mixture. Repeat six times, stacking layers. Do not butter the top layer. (If sheets break or tear, patch them with small pieces of phyllo.)

Arrange seafood lengthwise on lower third of phyllo sheets. Sprinkle with swiss cheese and chopped egg. Dot with sour cream *and sprinkle with $^{1}/4$ c. parsley, shallots, chives, and garlic. Dot with cream sauce.*

Tuck in ends of sheets and roll strudel jelly-roll fashion. Brush with melted butter. Strudel may be covered and refrigerated or frozen.

Bake in preheated oven at 375° for 12 minutes. Remove and brush with remaining butter. Bake an additional 35–40 minutes. Remove and brush again with butter. Allow strudel to stand 10 minutes. Dust with parmesan cheese and parsley. Serve in slices. Serves 6.

As long as you have decided to take on this much work, it would be worth making additional strudels and freezing some for future use.

Seafood
Strudel

from Los Abrigados

1 6-oz. piece of ahi tuna
15 nice beet leaves
5 spinach leaves
10 croutons
sorrel sauce
10 beet stems, washed and chopped

*S*eason and sear tuna to medium rare, then cut into strips.
Remove ribs from beet leaves, cut leaves into chiffonade by
rolling them together and slicing in 1/4" sections. Place 1 spinach
leaf on each plate. Top each with 1 crouton, then a touch of the
sauce. Stack chiffonade of beet leaves next, followed by 1 more
crouton, then tuna. Top with a bit more sauce and garnish plate
with beet stems.

Ahi Tuna Napoleon

CROUTONS

*Cut whole wheat bread into 10 2" circles. Mash
2 cloves of garlic and 1 piece of peeled ginger and
rub on bread circles. Chop 2 springs of thyme and
20 chives, and sprinkle over bread circles. Lightly
salt and pepper. Heat in 250° oven until dry and crisp.*

SORREL SAUCE

*In a blender, combine 2 oz. sorrel, 1 clove garlic, 1 shallot, 1 T.
wasabi powder, and 1/4 c. water. Add salt and pepper to taste.*

Poultry

Chicken Filling

This can be used for filling tacos, burritos, enchiladas, and tamales.

1 whole chicken (or chicken parts)
water to cover
1 T. poultry seasoning

Place chicken in a close-fitting pot. Cover with water and add poultry seasoning. Bring to boil, uncovered; then reduce heat to low, cover pot, and simmer about 20 minutes. Remove from heat, and allow pot to stand covered for about 2 hours. When pot is cool, skin and bone chicken. Divide chicken into 3-cup portions, and freeze in freezer bags.

Strain chicken broth, and chill. Then remove fat, and freeze in plastic containers. This is a great substitute for canned chicken broth.

Tortilla Casserole

This dish makes excellent use of leftover holiday turkey.

1 doz. corn tortillas, cut into 1" strips
2 1/2 c. shredded cheddar cheese
4 c. cooked turkey or chicken, cubed, shredded, or cut in strips
4 oz. sliced black olives
4 oz. chopped green chilies
16 oz. green chili salsa
1 can cream of mushroom soup
1 can cream of chicken soup
12 oz. chicken broth

Combine tortilla strips, 1 1/2 c. cheese, turkey, olives, chilies, salsa, soups, and broth. Pour into greased 9" x 13" casserole dish. Top with reserved 1 c. cheese, and bake at 350° for 45–60 minutes. Serve with salsa and sour cream. Serves 8.

1 c. water
1 pkg. taco seasoning mix
3 c. diced or shredded cooked chicken
2 green onions, sliced
16 oz. canned black beans, drained
1/4 c. chopped fresh cilantro
4 Flour Tortilla Baskets (page 37)
1 small head romaine lettuce, sliced, reserving a few leaves
1 tomato, peeled and diced
1 medium avocado, cut in thin wedges
1/4 c. sour cream
cilantro leaves for garnish

In a saucepan, bring water, taco seasoning, and chicken to a boil. Reduce heat and simmer 5 minutes. Stir in onion, black beans, and chopped cilantro. Crisp tortilla baskets in oven at 450° for 3 minutes. Cool. Place tortilla baskets on plates lined with sliced romaine leaves and surround with reserved romaine leaves. Spoon chicken mixture into tortilla baskets in equal portions. Top with tomato, avocado, and sour cream. Garnish with cilantro leaves and serve with favorite salsa. Serves 4.

Simple Tostados

1 T. curry powder
2 T. soy sauce
1/2 c. honey
1/2 c. dijon mustard
6 chicken breast halves, boned

*C*ombine curry powder, soy sauce, honey, and mustard. Place chicken pieces tightly in a baking dish, skin side down. Pour mixture over the top and refrigerate at least 6 hours to overnight. Turn chicken over, cover with foil, and place in oven preheated to 300°. Bake 30 minutes. Uncover chicken and baste with mixture from pan; cook an additional 15 minutes. Spoon sauce over chicken. Serves 6.

Absolutely
No-Work
Chicken

from La Mediterranée

4 chicken breasts
1 bunch fresh spinach
1 c. chopped mushrooms
2 T. pine nuts
1 c. feta cheese
dash salt and black pepper
$1/2$ c. white wine

Tenderize and flatten chicken breasts between two pieces of plastic wrap. Sauté spinach and mushrooms, add pine nuts, feta cheese, salt, and black pepper, and mix thoroughly. Stuff chicken breasts with this filling and fold. Place chicken in pan and pour wine over all. Cover with foil and bake at 375° for 20 minutes. Remove from pan and slice diagonally in 1"-wide pieces. Serve plain or with sauce. Serves 4.

SAUCE

Sauté 1 clove garlic and 1 c. diced mushrooms in $1/4$ c. white wine, add 1 t. green peppercorns, a dash each of salt and white pepper, and 1 c. heavy cream. Cook to reduce liquid. Pour over sliced stuffed chicken and serve.

Poule a la
Daniel

1 medium onion, chopped
2 cloves garlic, minced
1 T. oil
1 c. chicken broth
32 oz. canned great northern beans, drained
4 oz. diced green chilies
1 t. ground cumin
1/4 t. dried oregano, crushed
1/2 t. ground coriander
1/2 t. ground cloves
1/2 t. salt
cayenne pepper to taste
2 c. diced cooked chicken breast
1 1/2 c. grated jalapeño jack cheese

White Chili

In a large saucepan, cook onion and garlic in oil until soft, 5–10 minutes. Add broth, beans, chilies, cumin, oregano, coriander, cloves, salt, and cayenne pepper. Simmer 20 minutes. Add chicken; simmer 10 minutes. Serve in warm bowls and top with grated cheese. Serves 4 to 6.

Corn Husk Muffins (page 34) are a nice accompaniment to this dish. Shrimp, crab, or lobster may be substituted for the chicken.

These are usually served for brunch,
but they also make a great dinner entrée with salad.

2 bunches green onions, sliced
12 oz. cheddar cheese, grated
12 oz. jack cheese, grated
2 cans cream of chicken soup
1 pt. sour cream
8 oz. green chili strips
2 small cans sliced olives, drained
4 c. cubed cooked chicken breast
12 flour tortillas

Combine onion, cheeses, soup, sour cream, chilies, and olives to make sauce. Separate into two portions, and add chicken to one. Construct tortilla packets by placing 2–3 T. of the chicken-sauce mixture on each tortilla. Fold in half, and then in half the other way, forming a triangle. Trim about 1" from the top edge of each triangle with kitchen shears, and discard. Place triangles in a greased 9" x 13" casserole dish in overlapping layers. Cover with remaining sauce and bake at 350° for 45 minutes. Allow to stand for 10 minutes. Serve with chili verde sauce and sour cream. Serves 10 to 12.

Chicken Chalupas

Nice for brunch topped with scrambled eggs.

12 stale tortillas
(or spread fresh ones in a 200° oven for 20–30 minutes)
oil
salt
1 c. chopped onion
2 large tomatoes, peeled, seeded, and finely chopped
2 c. shredded cooked chicken
1/4 c. chicken broth
1 pkg. taco seasoning mix
14 oz. green chilies
1/2 c. sliced ripe olives
1 c. sour cream
1 c. shredded cheddar cheese

Chilaquiles

Cut tortillas into 3/4" strips. In a large skillet, fry strips in hot oil until chewy, but not crisp. Drain and salt lightly. In same skillet, cook onion in 1 T. oil until soft. Add tomatoes, chicken, broth, taco seasoning, chilies, and olives. Simmer uncovered for 10–15 minutes. Combine sauce with tortilla strips and spread in a greased flat 9" x 13" casserole dish. Spread sour cream on top, then sprinkle with cheese and additional pitted olives if desired. Bake uncovered at 375° for 20 minutes. Serves 6 to 8.

Shredded lettuce, chopped green onion, chopped cilantro, avocado slices, salsa, sour cream, and pitted ripe olives all make nice garnishes for this dish.

1 c. sun-dried cherries or cranberries
1/2 c. brandy
2 c. cooked wild rice
2 c. chopped celery
2 c. chopped onion
4 cloves garlic, minced
2 T. olive oil
1 T. minced crystallized ginger
1 T. crumbled dried sage (or 2 T. chopped fresh sage)
1 T. dried marjoram
1 egg, lightly beaten
12 oz. corn bread stuffing mix
salt and black pepper to taste
1/2–1 c. chicken broth

Submerge cherries or cranberries in brandy for 3 hours, then drain. Sauté celery, onion, and garlic in olive oil until soft. Combine with soaked dried fruit, rice, ginger, sage, marjoram, egg, stuffing mix, salt, and black pepper. Add enough chicken broth to moisten. Check seasonings and adjust if needed. Stuff chicken or turkey with dressing. Place any that won't fit in the bird in a greased casserole. Drizzle on a bit more chicken broth and dot with butter. Bake at 350° for 30 minutes.

Southwestern Poultry Dressing

You may have your favorite way to cook a turkey; my preference is to roast it breast side down, turning it over to brown the skin in the last hour of cooking.

10 chicken breast halves, skinned,
boned, and pounded thin
2 T. creole seasoning
1 c. chopped cilantro
4 T. olive oil
2 red peppers, 2 yellow peppers, 2 green peppers,
seeded and cut lengthwise in 1/4" slices
6 c. chicken broth
1 c. onion or shallot, minced
1 clove garlic, minced
2 T. olive oil
2 T. flour
8 oz. green salsa
4 oz. chopped green chilies
1 c. chicken broth

Rolled Chicken Breast

Season both sides of chicken breasts with creole seasoning and cilantro. Heat olive oil in skillet and sauté peppers over moderate heat for 4–5 minutes. Cut aluminum foil into ten 10" x 10" squares. Place one chicken breast on each piece of foil, and spoon pepper slices in equal portions over the chicken. Tightly roll each piece of chicken lengthwise with the peppers inside, and wrap in aluminum foil. In a large pot, bring chicken broth to a boil. Add foil-wrapped chicken. Cover and simmer for 15 minutes. Remove chicken and allow to cool. Remove foil.

In a skillet, sauté onion and garlic in olive oil for 2 minutes. Add flour and cook 2 more minutes. Add green salsa, chilies, and chicken broth, whisking until slightly thickened. Keep sauce warm. Cook chicken breast on preheated barbecue grill for 2 minutes per side. Remove and cut into 1/2" slices and serve with sauce. Serves 10.

Meats

This can be used for filling tacos, burritos, enchiladas, and tamales.

3 lbs. boneless chuck steak
1 t. salt
3 qts. cold water
1 onion, peeled and chunked
2 celery stalks, with leaves attached, chunked
2 carrots, chunked
3 sprigs of parsley

Combine beef, salt, and water in a large saucepan. Boil until foam forms. Skim foam from top and reduce heat. Add onion, celery, carrots, and parsley. Simmer, covered for 2 1/2 hours, or until meat is very tender. Remove beef and cool to room temperature. Shred beef by hand. (Beef may be frozen if desired.) Makes enough for at least 12 to 16 burritos.

Strain the remaining broth and reserve; when chilled, remove fat. This is good for cooking beans.

Shredded Beef Filling

from Oaxaca Restaurant and Cantina

6 oz. cubed top sirloin
3 c. water
1 clove fresh garlic
2 T. vegetable oil
1/2 chopped onion
1 lb. 12 oz. canned crushed tomatoes
4 diced tomatoes
1 t. crushed hot chili
1/2 t. garlic salt
1/2 t. oregano

Place sirloin, water, and garlic in pot, bring to a boil, and simmer with the lid on for 30 minutes. Cool and drain, reserving broth. When beef is cool enough to handle, shred by rolling between palms of hands into fine shreds. Heat oil and sauté onions until tender. Add canned tomatoes, diced tomatoes, chili, garlic salt, and oregano. Bring to a boil, add shredded beef and 2 c. of reserved broth; simmer for 30 minutes. This makes enough for burritos for 4 people.

Spicy Beef Filling

Use this for such dishes as Posolé (page 28) and tamales.

3 lb. pork shoulder roast
1 t. salt
1 bay leaf
1 t. dried sage

Place pork in a close-fitting pan and cover with water. Add salt, bay leaf, and sage. Bring to a boil, reduce heat, cover, and simmer for 2–3 hours. Turn off heat and allow to stand for 2 more hours. Remove pork from broth, drain on paper towels, cover and refrigerate both pork and broth overnight.

The next day, skim the hardened fat from broth and strain through a cheesecloth-lined strainer. Reserve broth for other uses (such as soups or cooking vegetables). Remove any visible fat and bones and discard. The pork is then ready to cube or shred as needed for the specific recipe. This makes enough for 12 enchiladas.

Shredding is easier if the pork is allowed to come to room temperature first.

Pork Filling

24 corn tortillas

oil

56 oz. canned enchilada sauce

28 oz. chicken broth

6 c. shredded cooked beef or pork (see previous recipes)

4 c. grated cheese (cheddar, jack, or both)

2 c. sliced green onions

1 c. sliced black olives

1 c. diced green chilies

P*our 2" oil in the bottom of a heavy skillet. Fry tortillas until slightly crisp; drain on paper towels. Bring enchilada sauce and chicken broth to a boil in large saucepan, reduce to simmer. Use tongs to hold crisp tortillas in sauce until slightly softened. Remove and cool. Combine the meat with 2 c. cheese. Place 1/4 c. of the meat-cheese mixture on each tortilla. Sprinkle with onions, olives, and chilies. Roll the filled tortillas and place seam-side down in two greased 9" x 13" casserole dishes. Cover with sauce. Sprinkle with remaining 2 c. cheese. Bake at 350° for 25–30 minutes. Serve with rice, beans, salsa, and steamed tortillas. Serves 12.*

Enchiladas

VARIATIONS

You can substitute chicken for the beef or pork. Or you can replace the meat-cheese filling with 8 c. shredded cheese. In this case, use 1/3 c. cheese in each tortilla.

I recommend making at least two dozen enchiladas at a time and freezing one dozen if necessary. They don't fall apart.

A great substitute for enchiladas if time is short.

1 1/2 lb. ground beef
3/4 t. ground cumin
1 T. chili powder
1 t. dried oregano
3 T. flour
16 oz. tomato sauce
10 oz. enchilada sauce
1/4 c. water
4 oz. chopped black olives
1 doz. corn tortillas, cut into 1" strips
3/4 c. chopped green onion
2 1/2 c. grated cheese (cheddar and/or jack)
4 oz. chopped black olives
1/2 c. chopped parsley

Enchilada Casserole

Sauté beef until brown; drain. Add cumin, chili powder, oregano, flour, tomato sauce, enchilada sauce, and water. Bring to a boil, add olives, and simmer 10 minutes. Spoon a layer of sauce into a greased 9" x 13" pan. Cover with half of the tortillas strips, half of the onions, and 3/4 c. cheese. Pour half of the remaining sauce over the top. Repeat process. Cover with remaining sauce and remaining cheese. Scatter olives and parsley over all. Bake for 45 minutes at 350°. Serves 8.

You can substitute 3–4 c. shredded chicken for the beef.

This dish goes way back.
It's always good for a brunch or light supper.

1 lb. ground beef
1 small onion, diced
$1/2$ t. dried basil, crushed
$1/4$ t. dried oregano, crushed
1 t. salt
$1/4$ t. black pepper
1 pkg. frozen chopped spinach, thawed and squeezed dry
4 eggs, beaten
4 oz. diced green chilies (optional)

B*rown meat and onion until crumbly. Stir in seasonings and squeezed spinach. Cook briefly over moderate heat until liquid has evaporated. Add eggs and chilies if desired. Cook, stirring frequently until eggs are set. Serves 4 generously.*

Jose's Especial

1/4 c. flour
1 T. chili powder
dash salt and black pepper
2 lbs. boneless pork, cut in 3" x 1/2" pieces
2 medium onions, diced
3 T. oil
1 T. tomato paste
2 T. soy sauce
1 can beef bouillon
1 lb. mushrooms, sliced
4 oz. diced green chilies
2 c. sour cream
1/4 c. minced cilantro

Southwestern Stroganoff

Combine flour, chili powder, salt, and black pepper. Dredge meat strips in flour mixture. Sauté onions in oil until soft. Add meat strips and sear. Add tomato paste, soy sauce, and bouillon, covering meat. Simmer for 2 hours. Before serving, reheat on low heat. Add mushrooms and green chilies, and simmer an additional 5 minutes. Add sour cream and simmer 5 more minutes. Serve over hot rice or noodles. Garnish with cilantro. Serves 6.

1 1/2 lb. boneless beef chuck, cut in 1" cubes
1 1/2 lb. boneless pork shoulder, cut in 1" cubes
3 T. olive oil
1 green pepper, chopped
1 clove garlic, minced
56 oz. canned crushed tomatoes
7 oz. canned chopped green chilies
1/2 c. chopped parsley
1/2 t. sugar
1/4 t. ground cloves
2 t. ground cumin
salt to taste
1 c. dry red wine

D ivide meat into fourths. Heat oil in large skillet, and brown meat on all sides, a fourth at a time. Remove meat to a plate using a slotted spoon. Add pepper and garlic to skillet and sauté, adding more oil if needed. Combine tomatoes, chilies, parsley, sugar, cloves, cumin, salt, and wine in a 5-quart pan. Bring mixture to a boil. Reduce to simmer, adding browned meat and sautéed vegetables.

Meaty Chili

Cover and simmer 2 hours, stirring occasionally. When ready to serve, sauce should be thick and meat tender. Adjust seasonings if necessary, and serve over rice or with tortillas. Serves 8 to 10.

Serve avocado, salsa, sour cream, and chopped cilantro as condiments to enhance this dish.

5 lbs. boneless chuck roast, fat removed
1 c. ketchup
1 c. barbecue sauce
1 c. water
1 onion, chopped
2 1/2 t. vinegar
2 t. worcestershire sauce
dash garlic powder
dash salt and black pepper

P lace meat in a roasting pan or dutch oven. Mix the remaining ingredients together and pour over the meat. Cover, place in oven, and cook at 300° for 5 hours or until meat becomes flaky and flakes into the sauce. Serve on crusty rolls. Serves 12 to 16.

Barbecue Beef

1 lb. ground beef
1/2 c. chopped onion
1 pkg. taco seasoning mix
4 oz. green chilies
2 1/2 oz. chopped black olives
3 eggs
1 1/4 c. milk
3/4 c. dry biscuit mix
2 tomatoes, peeled and diced
1 c. shredded cheese (cheddar and/or jack)

B*rown beef and onion; drain. Add taco seasoning and spread in a greased 8" x 8" glass dish or large pie plate. Cover with chilies and olives. Whisk eggs, milk, and biscuit mix together for 1 minute. Pour over beef mixture, and bake at 400° for 25 minutes, or until inserted knife comes out clean. Top with tomato and cheese, and allow dish to cool for 5 minutes. Cut in wedges or squares. Serve with chopped green onion and/or cilantro, sour cream, and salsa if desired. Serves 4 to 6.*

Impossible
Pie

from Poco Diablo Resort Hotel

6 2-oz. slices pork tenderloin, 1/4" thick
4 oz. flour
1 oz. butter
1/4 t. fresh ginger root
2 oz. white wine
1 stalk bok choy, sliced on the bias
3 oz. fresh orange juice
3 oz. sugar
6 orange slices, peeled, 1/4" thick
2 leaves of bok choy

Medallions of Pork Tenderloin with Bok Choy and Carmelized Oranges

Dust pork in flour. Melt butter in sauté pan; when hot, add pork and cook until golden; brown on both sides. Remove pork from pan and add ginger; sauté for 1 minute, then deglaze pan with white wine, and add bok choy slices and orange juice. Remove from heat, and set aside.

In separate pan, heat sugar until caramelized. Add orange slices and cook on each side. Then heat the orange juice and bok choy slices; add the pork, and cook for 1 minute.

Place 1 bok choy leaf on each plate, put pork atop leaf, then sliced bok choy and sauce from pan. Garnish with caramelized oranges. Serves 2.

Egg Dishes

from Oaxaca Restaurant and Cantina

1 T. butter
3 large eggs, beaten
4 oz. shredded beef
2 oz. shredded cheddar cheese
4 oz. green chili salsa

M*elt butter in omelet pan. Add eggs, and cook to desired omelet consistency. Sprinkle shredded beef and cheddar cheese over half of the cooked egg mixture. Fold the remaining half over the top to form omelet. Serve on platter with salsa on top. Serves 2.*

Eggs Oaxaca

from A Casalea

3 flour tortillas, cut into bite-sized pieces
1 c. enchilada sauce
1/2 c. cottage cheese
1 c. grated cheddar cheese
6 eggs
1/4 c. water
1/4 t. ground cumin
2 chopped green onions
light oil
chopped olives
chopped parsley

*S*pread tortilla pieces on bottom of ovenproof serving bowl. Mix together 1/2 c. enchilada sauce, cottage cheese, and 1/2 c. cheddar cheese. Heat in microwave 1 minute. Spread over tortilla pieces; set aside. Mix together eggs, water, cumin, and green onions. Scramble in oiled skillet over medium heat until fluffy. Spread eggs on top of cheese mixture. Pour remaining 1/2 c. enchilada sauce and 1/2 c. cheese on top. Put in hot oven just long enough to melt cheese. Top with olives and parsley. Serve hot. Serves 6 generously.

Easy
Enchilada
Eggs
Excellenté

6 corn tortillas
16 oz. refried beans
8 poached eggs
16 oz. salsa, heated in microwave
1/2 c. sliced green onions
1 c. shredded jack cheese
chopped cilantro (optional)

*P*reheat oven to 375°. Place tortillas in 1 or 2 greased flat baking dishes. Top with beans, eggs, salsa, onions, and cheese. Bake 10 minutes, or until cheese is melted. Serves 6 to 8.

If you don't have an egg poacher, fill a large flat saucepan two-thirds full of water, and bring to a boil. Reduce to moderate heat, and crack eggs carefully into the water, one at a time. Turn eggs with a large spoon so they take an oval form. When egg whites are set, remove with slotted spoon. If preparing ahead, place in a pan of cool water, cover, and store in the refrigerator until ready to use.

Almost-
Instant
Huevos
Rancheros

2 T. butter or margarine
7 oz. canned whole green chilies, seeded
(or 9 whole fresh chilies, roasted and seeded)
1/2 lb. jack cheese, shredded
1/4 lb. cheddar cheese, shredded
1 T. instant nonfat dry milk
1 c. buttermilk baking mix
1/2 t. salt
2 c. low-fat milk
1 T. oil
6 egg whites, lightly beaten

Melt butter in a 9" x 13" baking dish, tilting to cover the bottom. Place open chilies over butter. Combine cheeses and sprinkle over open chilies. Fold sides up and over cheese; chilies need not be completely closed. Combine dry milk, buttermilk baking mix, and salt, blend in oil and low-fat milk; fold in egg whites. Pour over chilies and bake uncovered at 350° for 40–45 minutes or until golden brown. Serves 6 to 8.

If using fresh chilies, place on top rack of oven 6" from heat. Turn oven to broil. Broil chilies, turning every few minutes, until peppers are dark brown and skin pops. Remove from oven and place in plastic bag until cool enough to handle (15–20 minutes). Pull off skins and slit to remove seeds.

This dish is great with Southwestern Coleslaw (page 44) and tamales.

Chilies Rellenos, Light Version

This dish must be prepared the day before.

5 slices sourdough bread
2 T. softened butter
3/4 lb. cheddar cheese, shredded
8 oz. green chilies, diced or in strips
4 eggs
2 T. dijon mustard
2 c. milk
salt and black pepper to taste

Chili Cheese Strata

*R*emove crusts from bread; butter the slices, and cut into cubes. Place cubes in an 8" x 8" greased baking dish. Cover with cheese and chilies. Whisk together eggs, mustard, milk, salt, and black pepper. Pour over bread cubes. Cover and refrigerate overnight. Bake at 350° for 45 minutes, or until nicely brown on top and an inserted knife comes out clean. Allow to stand for 10 minutes. Cut into 4" squares and serve with salsa and sour cream. Serves 4 to 6.

VARIATION

Add 1 lb. cooked and crumbled bacon or sausage or 1 lb. cooked and cubed ham.

This can be frozen before baking. To defrost, place on kitchen counter the night before serving.

1 1/2 c. chopped onion
4 T. oil
2 pkg. frozen chopped spinach, defrosted and squeezed dry
1/2 c. chopped green chilies
2 T. flour
2 c. milk
2 c. shredded jack cheese
1 t. crushed dried thyme
salt and black pepper to taste
6 eggs
1 c. shredded cheddar cheese
2 jalapeño peppers, finely diced (optional)
crumbled cooked bacon (optional)
6 tortillas (or 6 english muffin halves, toasted)

Hidden Eggs in Cheese and Spinach

Sauté onion in 2 T. oil until soft. Add squeezed spinach and chilies; cook 3 minutes and reserve. In a saucepan, mix flour with remaining 2 T. oil and cook until golden brown, 3–5 minutes. Slowly add milk, whisking until smooth, and cook until thickened. Add jack cheese, thyme, salt, and black pepper, continuing to cook until cheese is melted and sauce is smooth. Place spinach mixture in a greased 9" x 13" baking pan. Cover with cheese sauce. Using the back of a large spoon, form 6 wells in the sauce. Break an egg into each well and sprinkle with cheddar cheese. Top with jalapeños and/or bacon if desired. Bake at 350° for 20 minutes, or until eggs are set and cheese is melted. Divide and place each egg portion over a tortilla or toasted muffin. Serves 6.

Mixing cooked crumbled bacon or sausage or diced ham into the spinach mixture makes for a heftier version.

Vegetables

12 3" mushrooms, with stems removed
4 c. broccoli florets
1 T. lemon juice
1 can cream of broccoli soup
1/2 c. instant potato granules
1/4 c. grated parmesan cheese
3 T. softened butter
1 t. lemon juice
1/2 t. ground white pepper
1/8 t. ground nutmeg
1 T. snipped fresh dill (or 1 t. dried)
2 T. softened butter

Broccoli-Stuffed Mushrooms

In large saucepan, heat water to boiling. Drop in mushroom caps, and cook for 2 minutes. Remove to a bowl, using a slotted spoon. Then cook broccoli in same water until tender; drain. Gently toss mushrooms with 1 T. lemon juice, then drain. Blend cooked broccoli, soup, potato granules, cheese, 3 T. butter, 1 t. lemon juice, white pepper, nutmeg, and dill in a food processor. Spoon purée into mushroom caps. Dot caps with remaining butter. Bake at 450° for 10 minutes, or until golden brown. Serves 12.

These can also be refrigerated before baking for later use.

8–10 medium white onions
1 pkg. frozen spinach soufflé, defrosted
1/2 c. freshly grated parmesan cheese
white wine or beef broth

Spinach-Stuffed Onions

*P*lace onions in microwave and heat for 4–5 minutes until softened but not mushy, rotating once during cooking time. (Check occasionally for softness since microwave settings vary.) Slice off root end and gently peel onions, removing the centers, so a 1/2" shell remains. Fill centers with spinach soufflé. Cover with parmesan cheese and place in a greased 8" x 8" pan. Pour a small amount of wine or beef broth in bottom of pan. Bake at 350° for 45 minutes. Serves 8 to 10.

This dish can be baked ahead of time and reheated in a microwave.

These are different, delicate, and refreshing.

Braised Cucumbers

1 european cucumber, sliced into 1/8" slices
3 T. butter
salt and black pepper to taste
1/4 c. minced parsley

*G*ently sauté cucumber slices in butter until just tender. Salt and pepper to taste. Sprinkle with parsley and serve. Serves 4.

European cucumbers are the long, skinny ones that are usually wrapped in plastic in the market; they don't need to be peeled. If they are unavailable, you can use regular cucumbers; peel and seed them, then chop into 1" chunks.

Grated Braised Zucchini

8–10 small zucchini
2 T. salt
4 T. butter
salt and black pepper to taste

Grate zucchini (with skin intact) either by hand or in a food processor. Place in a large sieve and sprinkle with 2 T. salt, then toss to mix. Place weight on zucchini and allow to stand for 3 hours. Then rinse and squeeze zucchini dry with hands. Melt butter in a large skillet. Add zucchini and stir-fry until tender. Season with salt and black pepper. Serve as is or place in hollowed orange cups. Serves 6.

This recipe may also be used with other summer squashes.

Christmas Brussels Sprouts

1 1/2 lb. brussels sprouts,
trimmed, with an "X" cut in base
1 can beef broth
8 oz. dry white wine
(if additional liquid needed)
1 large red bell pepper, cut into 1/2" squares
3 T. butter

Place brussels sprouts and beef broth in a large skillet, and bring to a boil. Reduce heat and braise for 15–20 minutes, or until tender. Add white wine or additional broth if necessary. Turn sprouts occasionally until they are lightly browned and liquid has evaporated. Sauté bell pepper in butter in a medium skillet until softened. Place sprouts in a serving dish, and cover with pepper pieces. Serves 8.

If these won't be served immediately, cover them with plastic wrap, and microwave for 5–6 minutes to reheat.

2 c. yellow squash and/or zucchini,
cut into 1/2" cubes
2 cloves garlic, minced
2 medium tomatoes, peeled and diced
2 c. eggplant, peeled and cut into 3/4" cubes
3 medium onions, sliced
2 bell peppers (any color), sliced
1/2 t. dill seed
1/4 t. dried oregano
2 T. olive oil
salt and black pepper to taste

Ratatouille

*L*ayer vegetables in a greased casserole dish. Mix dill, oregano, oil, salt, and black pepper, and drizzle over vegetables. Bake uncovered at 350° for 1 hour. Serve hot or at room temperature. Serves 8 to 10.

64 oz. canned boston baked beans
(or pork and beans)
3/4 t. dry mustard
1/2 c. chili sauce
1 T. molasses
1/2 c. strong coffee
1/2 c. bourbon
12 slices canned pineapple
brown sugar

Bourbon
Beans

*C*ombine beans, mustard, chili sauce, molasses, coffee, and bourbon, and place in a baking dish. Allow to stand for at least 3 hours. Bake covered at 350° for 40 minutes. Remove cover, top with sliced pineapple, then sprinkle with brown sugar. Bake uncovered for 40 more minutes. Serves 12 easily.

1 lb. black beans
2 large onions, minced
1/2 c. olive oil
6 cloves garlic, minced
1 t. salt
4 bay leaves
3 T. chili powder
2 ham hocks
1 t. dried oregano
2 t. ground cumin
8 oz. tomato sauce

Black Beans

Wash beans and soak in water overnight. Sauté onion in oil until tender. Add garlic and sauté 2 more minutes. Drain beans and place in a large pot with 2 qts. water. Add remaining ingredients and cook over low heat until beans are tender, about 2 1/2 hours; add additional water if necessary. To test for doneness, remove a few beans and blow on them; the beans are done if the skins rise up. When beans are tender, remove ham hocks and bay leaves. Trim out the lean ham meat, and return it to the beans. Serves 6.

Try serving this dish with Corn Pancakes (page 36) instead of the usual tortillas.

1/2 c. finely chopped green onions
1 1/2 c. sliced black olives
2 T. butter
2 T. flour
2 1/2 c. milk
4 eggs, well beaten
2 t. salt
2 t. sugar
1 t. dry mustard
1/4 t. white pepper
4 c. fresh corn kernels
1 1/2 c. soft bread crumbs
1 c. shredded cheddar cheese
1/4 c. chopped parsley

Ripe Olive Corn Pudding

In a large saucepan, sauté onions and olives in butter over low heat for 5 minutes. Stir in flour and cook 3 minutes. Slowly add milk, stirring until mixture thickens; remove from heat. In a bowl, combine eggs, salt, sugar, mustard, and pepper, and add to olive mixture. Add corn, bread crumbs, cheese, and parsley. Turn into 2 1/2–qt. greased baking dish. Place in a larger dish of hot water so the water rises halfway up the side. Place in oven and bake at 350° for 70 minutes, or until mixture is firm in the center and a knife inserted in the center comes out clean. Serves 8.

This dish is nice with barbecued meats as an alternative to potatoes.

Riz Autentico

1 c. long-grained rice
1/2 c. lard
2 1/2 c. chicken broth
1 tomato, peeled, seeded, and diced
1/2 c. diced onion
salt to taste

In a saucepan, fry rice in lard until golden brown. Add broth and bring to a boil. Add tomato, onion, and salt. Cover and simmer for 25 minutes. Serves 6.

Perfect every time!

Hot Jalepeño Rice

from A Casalea

2 c. brown rice
2 or 3 finely chopped
canned jalapeño peppers
1 T. jalapeño juice
1/2 t. ground cumin
salt to taste
4 T. butter
small tomato slices
parsley sprigs

Cook rice, drain, and rinse. Add peppers, jalapeño juice, cumin, and salt. Top with butter. Heat in oven or microwave until butter is melted. Mix lightly. Garnish with tomato and parsley. Serve hot. Serves 6.

Foul Medammas
(Fava Beans)

from La Mediterranée

This recipe won grand prize at the Arizona Garlic Festival in 1991.

2 c. dried fava beans
1 t. baking soda
1 medium onion, chopped
2 cloves fresh garlic, mashed
2 tomatoes, diced
juice of 1 lemon
2 T. olive oil
dash salt and black pepper

Cover beans with water, add baking soda, and soak covered overnight. Drain the next day, cover with fresh water, and boil for 1 hour, or until tender. Drain, add remaining ingredients, and mix thoroughly until half the beans are broken. Serves 4.

Low~Calorie Oven~Baked Fries

3 potatoes, unpeeled
1 1/2 t. oil
1 T. water
salt

Cut each potato into 10–12 wedges. Shake wedges in a bag containing oil and water. Place on baking sheet sprayed with nonstick vegetable spray, and bake at 375° for 40 minutes, turning 3–4 times while baking. The potatoes should be somewhat crispy. Sprinkle with salt and serve. Serves 4.

1 1/2 lb. unpeeled new potatoes,
sliced into 1/8" slices
salt and freshly ground black pepper
3/4 c. heavy cream
1/2 c. chicken broth
1 c. shredded swiss cheese

P lace potatoes in a greased 9" x 9" casserole dish. Sprinkle with
salt and black pepper. Combine cream and chicken broth,
and pour over potatoes. Cover and bake at 350° for 30 minutes.
Uncover and bake 30 more minutes. Sprinkle with cheese, and
bake uncovered until cheese is melted and bubbly. Serves 6.

Cheesy
Potatoes

These can be prepared ahead and baked just before serving.

8 medium russet potatoes, peeled and chunked
dash salt
I clove garlic, minced
2 egg yolks, beaten
3/4 c. cream
1/4 c. butter, melted
salt and black pepper to taste
1/4 c. chopped parsley

*C*ook *potatoes and garlic in water until tender. Drain and mash. Combine eggs, cream, butter, salt, black pepper, and parsley. Fold into potatoes, and place in a greased casserole dish. Bake at 350° for 30 minutes, or until browned.*
Serves 8.

VARIATION

Substitute 8 oz. cream cheese for the butter and cream. Or add 1/2 lb. sautéed sliced mushrooms or 2 c. minced green ripe olives.

Baked Mashed Potatoes

Salsas and Sauces

Nopalitos Salsa

Yes, nopalito means cactus! Prickly pear cactus!

16 oz. nopalitos, diced and drained
8 oz. canned or fresh roasted chilies, diced
16 oz. tomatillos, drained (or 2 lbs. fresh)
1 c. finely chopped white onion
1/4 c. chopped fresh cilantro
3–4 canned jalapeño peppers, finely diced
3 T. white vinegar
1 T. salt

Combine all ingredients and refrigerate. This salsa will keep for up to two weeks.

If you use fresh tomatillos, remove their paper-like husks, and simmer in water until soft. Drain and crush.

Fresh nopalitos can be purchased in many supermarkets. To pre-pare them, use a strawberry picker to pick out the brown spots where the cactus spines were. Trim off the edges and dice. Cover with water and simmer until tender. Drain and rinse, rinse, rinse, and rinse again to remove the syrupy substance that the cactus secretes.

Mango Pineapple Salsa

1 mango or papaya, diced
1/2 c. finely chopped white onion
1 c. diced fresh pineapple
1/4 c. chopped cilantro
4 oz. diced green chilies
3–4 dashes hot pepper sauce

Combine all ingredients and refrigerate. This salsa will keep in the refrigerator up to three days.

*Served with turkey, this makes a nice change
from cranberry sauce.*

**Cranberry
Salsa**

12 oz. fresh cranberries, washed
1 small white onion, chunked
1/2 c. parsley leaves
4 oz. green chilies, diced
2–3 jalapeño chilies, diced (optional)
2 t. grated orange zest
2 t. lemon juice
1/4 c. orange juice
3 T. honey
salt to taste

*Combine cranberries, onion, and parsley in a food processor,
and chop fine. Add remaining ingredients and refrigerate
at least 4 hours. This salsa will keep in the refrigerator for two
to three days.*

1/2 c. dried cherries
1/2 c. cranberry juice
12 oz. fresh cranberries, washed
1/2 c. brown sugar
1/4 t. vanilla

**Triple
Cranberry
Sauce**

*Combine cherries and cranberry juice in a
2-qt. glass container. Microwave on high for 2 minutes.
Stir in fresh cranberries and sugar. Cover and microwave on high
for 5–7 minutes, stirring twice. Continue cooking until sauce
thickens. Add vanilla, stir, and allow to cool.*

This sauce may be prepared one week in advance.

Fruit Chutney

4 lbs. pears, peaches, nectarines, or plums
(or combination), seeded, peeled and chopped
2 large cloves garlic, minced
2 t. hot paprika (or 1 t. cayenne pepper)
2 t. ground coriander
1 c. vinegar (or lime juice, or combination)
1 1/2 c. golden raisins
3 T. minced fresh ginger
1 1/2 c. brown sugar
8 oz. green chilies, diced

Cook fruit, garlic, paprika, coriander, vinegar, raisins, and ginger, until fruit is tender. Add sugar and cook about 10 minutes, or until sludgy in texture, not liquid. Fold in chilies and pour into sterilized 8-oz. jars. This can be refrigerated indefinitely.

Anaheim Chutney

from Enchantment Resort

8 oz. fresh anaheim chilies, roasted, peeled,
and diced (or 8 oz. canned diced chilies)
1/2 c. sugar
1/2 t. diced shallots
1/4 c. cider vinegar
1/2 t. cumin
1/2 t. salt

Mix all ingredients in a saucepan, and bring to a boil. Reduce heat and simmer while stirring until syrupy in texture. Serve at room temperature.

This chutney is good with grilled fish or chicken. It also makes a great appetizer when poured over a block of cream cheese and served with crackers. It will keep in the refrigerator indefinitely.

1 1/2 c. dry mustard
1 1/2 c. white vinegar
3 eggs, beaten
1 1/2 c. sugar

Mustard Sauce

*C*ombine mustard and vinegar; let stand overnight. Add eggs *and sugar. Cook in double boiler until slightly thickened. Will keep two to three weeks.*

from Oaxaca Restaurant and Cantina

Green Chili Sauce

2 T. vegetable oil
1/2 c. chopped onion
6 oz. diced green chilies
3/4 t. garlic powder
1/2 t. salt
1/4 t. oregano
1/2 c. diced tomato
12 oz. water
2 T. vegetable oil
4 oz. unbleached flour

*H*eat oil, add onion, and sauté until soft. Add chilies, garlic *powder, salt, oregano, tomato, and water. Bring to boil, then simmer 10 minutes. Heat oil and add flour to make a roux. Add vegetable mixture, stirring constantly. Boil until sauce is thickened.*

1/2 c. flour
1/4 c. chili powder
1/4 c. paprika
4 c. chicken broth

*C*ombine flour, chili powder, and paprika in a saucepan. Add chicken broth to moisten. Place over medium heat, stirring and cooking until thickened. Add broth to thin to desired consistency.

This sauce can also be used for burritos or chilies rellenos.

Enchilada Sauce

Desserts

This is lovely to serve at brunch or after a heavy meal.

1 cantaloupe, diced or scooped into balls
1 honeydew melon, diced or scooped into balls
1/4 small watermelon (seedless is best),
diced or scooped into balls
1 c. seedless grapes
1 c. blueberries
2/3 c. sugar
1/3 c. water
2 t. lime zest
6 T. lime juice
1/2 c. rum
mint sprigs
1 c. sliced strawberries
(or whole small berries)

Fruit in Rum-Lime Sauce

Combine melons, grapes, and blueberries; chill. Bring sugar and water to a boil; simmer 5 minutes. Add lime zest, and cool to room temperature. Stir in lime juice and rum. Pour sauce over chilled fruit, and continue chilling for several hours. Garnish with mint sprigs and strawberries. Serves 8.

4 large oranges (or 3 cans mandarin oranges)
2 large mangoes (or papayas)
vanilla ice cream
8-10 Dessert Tortilla Baskets (page 37),
sprinkled with sugar and cinnamon
before baking
I jar caramel topping

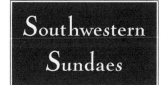

Southwestern Sundaes

*P*eel oranges with a sharp knife so no white pith is left; then hold fruit over a bowl to catch juices and slice next to each membrane, down and up, to remove orange segments. Dice mangos (or papayas), and combine with orange segments. Chill for 8 hours. Place a generous scoop of ice cream in each tortilla cup. Spoon fruit mixture on top. Heat caramel sauce in microwave, and drizzle over fruit. Serves 8 to 10.

For a simple dessert, serve this with coffee after a large meal.

Dessert Brie

1/2 c. brown sugar
1/2 c. chopped toasted pecans
I T. orange liqueur
I 6-oz. brie cheese
I pkg. cookie wafers

*C*ombine sugar, nuts, and liqueur. Remove top rind from cheese and discard; cover cheese with nut mixture. Place on ovenproof serving plate, and bake at 350° for 15–20 minutes. Serve with cookie wafers. Serves 6.

2" freshly peeled ginger, sliced
1/4 c. water
6 egg yolks
1 c. sugar
2 c. half-and-half
2 c. whipping cream

*B*lend ginger and water in a blender at high speed for 2 minutes. Strain liquid through cheesecloth; set aside. In a saucepan over medium heat, whisk egg yolks and sugar for 5 minutes, or until thick and pale yellow. In the microwave, scald half-and-half for 4–5 minutes. Whisk half-and-half slowly into egg yolks, turn heat to high, and continue whisking until mixture is slightly thickened, about 3 minutes. Stir in ginger mixture and chill for 2 hours. Add unwhipped whipping cream; chill again. Place in ice cream maker and process according to manufacturer's instructions. Serves 6.

Ginger Ice Cream

Another intriguing gift.

1 c. butter (2 sticks)
4 oz. cream cheese
4 oz. processed cheese spread, plain
1/2 c. powdered cocoa
2 lbs. powdered sugar
1 c. chopped nuts (or more)
2 t. vanilla

P*lace butter and cheeses in a 2-qt. bowl, and melt in microwave, stirring until blended. Stir in cocoa. Gradually add powdered sugar, blending until mixture is smooth. Add vanilla and nuts. Spread in a 9" x 9" pan. Chill. Cut into 64 squares.*

Surprise
Fudge

This dessert is particularly good following a Mexican meal.

1 1/4 c. brown sugar
2 c. boiling water
1/3 c. cornstarch
1/4 c. cool water
3 egg whites, beaten
1 t. almond extract
3 egg yolks
1/2 c. sugar
1 T. cornstarch
2 c. milk
1 t. vanilla
grated nutmeg

Cielito Pudding

*S*tir brown sugar into boiling water. Mix cornstarch and cool water, add to brown sugar mixture, and cook over medium heat until thickened, about 15 minutes. Cool slightly. Pour over beaten egg whites, add almond extract, and fold gently. Chill.

To prepare custard sauce, whisk together egg yolks, sugar, and cornstarch. Add to milk and cook over medium heat, continuing to whisk until thickened. Stir in vanilla. Scoop pudding into individual bowls, and top with custard sauce. Sprinkle with grated nutmeg. Serves 6 to 8.

1 c. sugar
1 qt. milk
1 pt. half-and-half
6 large eggs
6 T. sugar
2 t. vanilla
dash salt
freshly grated nutmeg

M*elt sugar in a small saucepan over medium heat, stirring and watching constantly, until caramel colored. Quickly pour into a soufflé dish, and roll melted sugar around the inside of dish until the bottom and 2" of the sides are completely covered. Set aside.*

In microwave, scald milk and half-and-half together for about 6 minutes. Beat eggs with sugar, vanilla, and salt. Combine with scalded milk, and pour over soufflé dish. Sprinkle grated nutmeg on top.

Place soufflé dish in a pan filled with enough water that the water covers the bottom third of the soufflé dish. Place in oven and bake at 350° for 1 hour. Check center for doneness with a steel knife. If knife comes clean, flan is done. Leave soufflé dish in oven with door slightly ajar for 2 hours. Then refrigerate.

Nana's
Flan

Before serving, run the blade of a knife around the edge of the soufflé dish. Place a serving plate on top of the soufflé dish, and invert. You now have a lovely flan surrounded by caramel sauce. Serves 8 to 10.

1 c. sugar
1/2 c. melted butter
1 c. flour
1/4 t. salt
1 t. ground cinnamon
1/4 t. ground nutmeg
1 c. puréed persimmon pulp
(from 3 to 4 persimmons)
2 t. baking soda
2 t. warm water
3 T. brandy
1 t. vanilla
2 eggs, lightly beaten
1 c. golden raisins
1/2 c. chopped walnuts or pecans
1/4 c. brandy

Persimmon Pudding

Mix sugar and butter. Sift flour with salt, cinnamon, and nutmeg; add to butter-sugar mixture, then blend in persimmon pulp. Dissolve baking soda in warm water, and add to pudding, along with brandy, vanilla, eggs, raisins, and nuts. Turn into a greased 5–6 cup mold. Cover with foil or mold lid, and place on steamer rack of a large kettle with enough water to rise halfway up the side of mold. Bring water to a boil, cover kettle, reduce heat and simmer for 3 hours. Allow to stand for 30 minutes before removing from mold. Unmold pudding on a serving dish. Heat 1/4 c. brandy in microwave for 20 seconds. Ignite and pour over pudding. Serves 8.

After pudding is steamed, it can be refrigerated for several days or frozen. Before serving, bring pudding to room temperature by warming in oven, covered loosely with an aluminum foil "tent" at 250° for 30 minutes, or by unmolding and then microwaving the loosely covered pudding for 5 minutes.

1/2 c. flour
1/2 c. brown sugar
1/3 c. butter
3/4 c. rolled oats
4 medium granny smith apples, peeled and chopped
1 1/2 c. fresh cranberries
1/2 c. sugar
2 T. flour
1 t. cinnamon

M*ix together flour, brown sugar, butter, and rolled oats; set aside. Combine apples, cranberries, sugar, flour, and cinnamon. Place fruit in a microwave pan, and sprinkle rolled oat mixture on top. Microwave on high heat for 12–14 minutes, rotating dish every 4 minutes. Serve warm with vanilla ice cream. Serves 6.*

Apple Cranberry Crisp

An unusual dessert you'll be glad you tried.

1/2 c. butter, softened
1/4 c. sugar
1 c. cornmeal
2 eggs, at room temperature
1 t. salt
1 1/2 c. flour
2/3 c. heavy cream
24 oz. ricotta cheese
1 c. sugar
3 eggs
1 T. lemon zest
1/4 c. lemon juice
1/2 t. crushed dried thyme
3 T. flour

Lemon Thyme Tart

Beat together butter and sugar. Add cornmeal, eggs, and salt, and beat until smooth. Add flour, and mix until dough forms a ball. Cover with plastic wrap, and chill 1 hour. Then roll out to fit in a 9" springform pan with the crust coming up slightly on the sides. Prick with a fork several times. Bake at 350° for 8 minutes, or until slightly brown.

Combine cream, cheese, sugar, eggs, lemon zest, lemon juice, thyme, and flour, beating until smooth. Pour filling into crust, and bake at 350° until filling is set and lightly browned, about 1 hour. Turn oven off and allow tart to stand in oven for 30 minutes. Cool, cover, and chill.

At serving time, remove sides of pan, and cut into 10 wedges. Garnish each serving with edible flowers such as violets, pansies, or nasturtiums. Serves 10.

A great gift, and easy to make.

1 c. sugar
1/2 c. white corn syrup
1 c. whole almonds (with skins)
1 t. butter
1 t. vanilla
1 t. baking soda

P*lace sugar and corn syrup in 1 1/2–qt. microwave dish.
Microwave on high 4–5 minutes (longer during cold weather).
Add almonds. Microwave 3–5 minutes, or until light brown. Add
butter and vanilla. Microwave 1–2 minutes more. Add baking soda.
Stir until light and foamy. Quickly pour on nonstick or buttered
cookie sheet. Cool 45 minutes. Break up and store in airtight cans.
Makes 1 pound.*

Almond Brittle

*These also make great gifts. They can be prepared ahead
and frozen until gift-giving time.*

16 oz. semisweet baking chocolate
2/3 c. sweetened condensed milk
1 T. chocolate-coffee liqueur
1/4 t. almond extract
cocoa
chopped macadamia nuts or chopped toasted
blanched almonds (optional)

Melt chocolate in a heavy 2-qt. saucepan over low heat. Remove from heat, and stir in condensed milk, liqueur, and almond extract. Refrigerate about 40 minutes. Dust hands with cocoa. Scoop out fudge with a teaspoon, and roll into balls. Roll each ball in cocoa and, if desired, chopped nuts. Pack in individual paper candy cups, and then place in boxes or tins. Makes 36.

Mocha Truffles

VARIATION

Substitute 1 T. raspberry liqueur for the chocolate-coffee liqueur. Roll each ball carefully around a frozen raspberry.

3 eggs
2/3 c. sugar
I c. light corn syrup
3 T. melted butter
I t. vanilla
I 1/2 c. chopped macadamia nuts
I prepared pie shell

*C*ombine eggs, sugar, corn syrup, butter, and vanilla. Add nuts, and pour mixture into pie shell. Bake at 350° for 45 minutes, or until filling is set (test with knife). Cool on a wire rack.

Macadamia
Nut Pie

8 eggs
9 oz. butter, softened
1 lb. chocolate
1 c. finely chopped macadamia nuts
1/2 c. sugar
1 t. cream of tartar
powdered sugar

Separate egg yolks and whites. Add butter to yolks and beat until incorporated. Melt chocolate in double boiler and add to butter mixture. Fold in macadamia nuts. Whip whites until frothy; slowly add sugar and cream of tartar, and beat to medium peaks. Fold one-third of the whites into the chocolate mixture. Gently fold in the remaining whites. Pour batter into a buttered and floured 9" spring-form pan. Bake at 400° for 45 minutes. Cool. Sprinkle top with powdered sugar. Serves 10 to 12.

Macadamia Chocolate Cake

3 oz. butter

1/2 c. sugar

3/4 t. vanilla

1/8 t. salt

1/4 c. + 2 T. sifted unsweetened cocoa powder

3/4 c. flour

1 1/4 c. heavy cream

10 oz. bittersweet chocolate, chopped into small pieces

In food processor, combine butter, sugar, vanilla, and salt; process until creamy. Add cocoa, and process until mixture is a dark smooth paste. Add flour and pulse until incorporated but crumbly. Knead on counter. Pat into circular disk. Chill in refrigerator 30 minutes. Roll out between two pieces of wax paper, and place in 9 1/2" tart pan. Prick all over. Bake at 375° for 12–14 minutes. Cool on rack.

In small saucepan, bring cream to a simmer over medium heat. Add chocolate, and stir very gently until chocolate melts and mixture is smooth. Pour mixture through fine strainer into chocolate tart shell. Refrigerate 3–4 hours before serving.

Bittersweet Chocolate Tart

This recipe has been handed down for many years on Fran's father's family. (He arrived in the United States from England in the 1930s.) This trifle is fabulous for Easter, Mother's Day, or other special springtime festivities.

CAKE

1 c. sifted flour
1 t. baking powder
1/4 t. salt
1/2 c. milk
2 T. butter
2 eggs
1 c. sugar
2 t. vanilla

CUSTARD

1/3 c. sugar
1 T. cornstarch
1/8 t. salt
1 c. milk
2 beaten egg yolks
1 T. butter
2 t. vanilla
1/2 c. whipping cream

TOPPING

3 pts. strawberries
3 T. sugar
1/3 c. high-quality orange liqueur
powdered sugar
whipped cream

Fran Bruno's
Old English
Trifle

To make cake, sift together flour, baking powder, and salt in a large bowl. In small saucepan, heat milk and butter until *butter melts; keep hot. In mixer bowl, beat eggs at high speed until thick, about 3 minutes. Gradually add sugar, beating constantly at medium speed for 4–5 minutes. Add sifted dry ingredients to egg mixture. Stir until just blended. Add hot milk mixture and vanilla; blend well. Turn into 2 greased and floured 8" round cake pans. Bake at 350° for 20 minutes. Cool.*

To prepare custard, combine sugar, cornstarch, and salt in a saucepan. Stir in milk. Cook and stir over medium heat until thick and bubbly. Stir moderate amount of hot mixture into egg yolks to warm them. Then combine yolks with mixture in pan, stirring constantly. Cook and stir 2 more minutes; remove from heat. Stir in butter and vanilla. Cover surface of custard with waxed paper or clear plastic. Chill. Beat whipping cream until stiff, and fold into chilled pudding. Set aside.

To prepare topping, crush strawberries to make 2 cups—after setting aside 14 of the best berries for garnish. Stir in sugar, and set aside.

To assemble the trifle, make four cake layers by cutting both cakes in half horizontally. Fit one bottom layer into the bottom of a large glass bowl; spread 1 c. berry mixture over cake. Top with second cake layer, cut side up; sprinkle half of the liqueur over the cut side, and spread with all of the custard mixture. Place third layer atop custard and spread with remaining berry mixture. Sprinkle cut side of top layer with remaining liqueur and place it, cut side down, atop berries. Cover and refrigerate.

Right before serving, sift powdered sugar on top of trifle. Score top with X's. Garnish with whipped cream and reserved strawberries. Serves 12 to 16.

**Fran Bruno's
Old English
Trifle**

Do not use substitutes for the cake or custard layers. Making everything from scratch is a bit of work, but well worth the effort. The cake is super light, the custard nothing like any store-bought variety. It is best to make the parts the day ahead, and assemble the trifle at the last minute.

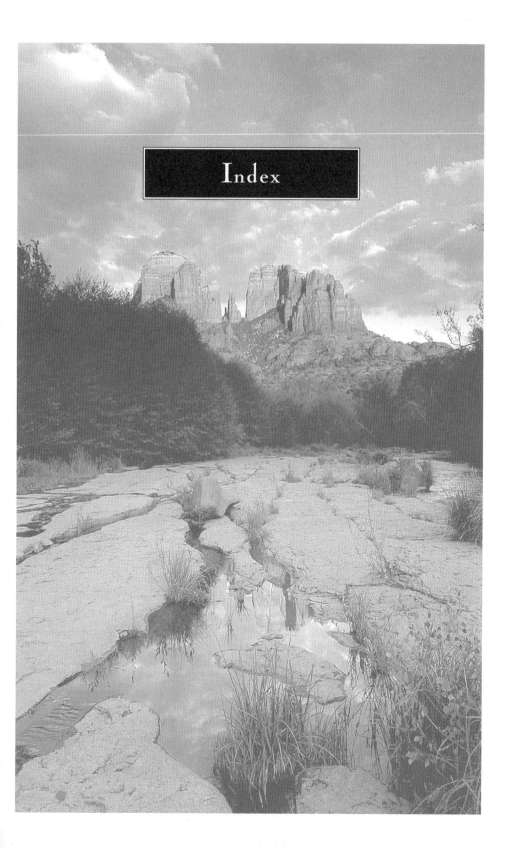

Index

Photograph by Richard Hogeland

E loise Carleton, a Southern California trans-
plant, moved to Sedona four years ago after
being infected with a common malady, "Red Rock
Fever," while visiting. She admits she could not
fry an egg at the time of her marriage in the 1950s,

Eloise
Carleton

but the culinary influences of a French grandmother, a mother-in-
law in the restaurant business, and her own mother, eldest of ten,
finally had their impact. Eloise learned to cook, and she now loves
to entertain. In addition to serving guests, she also serves on the
boards of directors of the Sedona Museum of Art and the Sedona
Flagstaff Symphony League—it was at one of their dinners that
she realized there were no Sedona cookbooks on the market, and
Red Rock Recipes was conceived.